I WILL FIND YOU

I WILL FIND YOU

DAPHNE BENEDIS-GRAB

SCHOLASTIC INC.

ISBN 978-1-338-88474-6

10 9 8 7 6 5 4 3 2 1   23 24 25 26 27

Printed in the U.S.A.   40

First edition, October 2023

Book design by Maeve Norton

FOR SARA

PART 1

**Snippet from the Snow Valley Police
Department Log
Missing Persons Case 3125
Time: 7:04 a.m.
Interview subject: Grace O'Brian, 12 years
old, accompanied by mother, Lydia O'Brian
Cabinmate of Nicholas Finley**

SERGEANT WILLIAMS:

*What were your impressions of Nicholas's mental
state when you first arrived at Frost Peak
Campground?*

GRACE:

*Um, I don't know. Maybe he was excited? Most
people were—everyone gets pretty psyched about the
seventh-grade campout. But I didn't talk to him or
anything.*

SERGEANT WILLIAMS:

When did you first interact with Nicholas?

GRACE:

*I didn't really. He was assigned to my cabin and
stuff, but I just dropped off my backpack and then
left for the mess hall to eat. And we didn't have to*

sit with our cabinmates at dinner or the campfire.

So I was with my friend the whole time.

SERGEANT WILLIAMS:

Which means the first time you saw Nicholas was at
curfew when everyone returned to their cabins for
the night?

GRACE:

Kind of. But he was already asleep. Or at least he
was in his bunk in his sleeping bag, and he didn't
say anything when I went through. I was on the
other side, with Olivia. So I just said hi to Ms.
Becker and she closed the partition thing because
Olivia was already there.

SERGEANT WILLIAMS:

And then in the morning?

GRACE (VISIBLY AGITATED):

In the morning he was gone. His sleeping bag was
empty and Nicky was gone.

CHAPTER 1

GRACIE

The crowded school bus turned onto a dirt road, then thumped over a pothole. Thick, dark forest closed in on either side.

"We're here!" someone shouted, and a big cheer went up around Gracie as the bus bounced its way toward the parking lot of Frost Peak Campground.

As Gracie's best friend, Mina, clapped happily, Gracie tried to join in the excitement. Who wouldn't be excited for the annual seventh-grade camping trip? There were the nightly campfires with s'mores, the Saturday ropes course over Coldwater Creek, and the sunset hike.

Frost Peak Campground was only thirty minutes outside town, and a twenty-minute bike ride on Kappa Path, which wound through the woods. Gracie and Mina had been there a million times, if not more—for Fourth of July fireworks, summer barbecues, and day camp when they were little. Gracie and Mina did everything together, always.

Until now.

Gracie could feel the smile fade from her face.

"I hate that we're not together, Gracie-cakes," Mina said, seeming to sense Gracie's mood and stretching up to loop an arm around Gracie's neck. It was a challenge because Gracie had recently had a huge growth spurt, while Mina had remained petite. But it still felt good to have her friend's arm around her. "It's not fair they separated us."

Gracie agreed, quite fervently. How would she enjoy the trip on her own?

"Remember, it's just two nights," Mina said, giving Gracie a soft squeeze, clearly knowing what Gracie was thinking. "And we'll be together during the day—"

"But the cabin is the best part," Gracie moaned. Just then the bus hit a particularly deep pothole, which caused Gracie's backpack to bounce off the floor, slamming into her shins. "Staying up late and talking after the cabin chaperone goes to sleep. It's like the world's best sleepover."

"Other parts are good too," Mina said optimistically, because she was always optimistic.

"At least you got fun bunkmates," Gracie said, knowing she was sulking but unable to help herself. Mina had an easier time talking to other people than Gracie did to begin with, and Mina's cabin had three of the sweetest girls in the grade so she would be fine. They would have a good time together. Meanwhile, Gracie was stuck with Olivia and Jessica.

"You didn't get the *best* people," Mina acknowledged. "Olivia's not bad exactly, she's just—"

"Olivia," Gracie finished with a sigh. Olivia wasn't bad—she was intimidating and that was worse. Olivia was the coolest girl in seventh grade, possibly the coolest girl in the school, partly because she didn't know it and wouldn't care if she found out. Her parents owned Exceptional People, a comic book store, and Olivia knew all there was to know about graphic novels, superheroes (in books, on TV, and in movies), and manga. If that wasn't cool enough, she was the fastest skater in school (that included the high school) and wore clothes that were the perfect combination of pure fashion and pure Olivia. But what really made her intimidating was that she said whatever she felt like saying and never once worried what anyone thought.

The only thing Gracie had in common with Olivia was that they were both human beings.

"But she's nice—or at least she's not mean," Mina said. "And Jessica's not awful—she always helps me in tech class. She's just kind of a loner."

That was the truth. Jessica had never been hugely social—plus last spring there had been that incident with her hair—and then she had gotten super into computers, so good that Mr. Simmons, the tech teacher, often asked her to help out during their class and at lunch when kids came in to finish assignments. She was basically the aide of the computer lab and was there anytime she wasn't in class. And while Mina was comfortable with Jessica's blunt manner, Gracie avoided her—she had a way of explaining things that made Gracie feel dumb. Gracie was hoping to get the second bedroom to herself but it was unlikely—Olivia or Jessica would be quick to claim it.

Just then the bus pulled to a halt at the main lodge of Frost Peak Campground. The Catskill Mountains, dappled in late-afternoon sunlight, framed the big wooden building where they would eat their meals.

All the kids stood up, grabbed their bags, and pushed toward the exit, eager to get outside and officially begin the campout. Mina stepped into the aisle, Gracie following close behind. As reluctant as she was to be separated from Mina, she was eager to get off the bus, which smelled of old ham and sour milk laced with a whiff of puke. Gracie had always had an extra-good sense of smell and at times like this it was a bit of a curse.

"Move it," someone snapped from the back of the bus. Gracie did not need to turn to see who it was—everyone in the seventh grade knew Nicky Finley's voice. That was what happened when you had been the longtime bully of pretty much everyone in the class.

"Jerk," Gracie heard someone ahead of her hiss. Though not loudly enough to be heard all the way back to where Nicky was standing—no one wanted to tangle with someone that mean. Including Gracie and Mina, who hurried out.

A throng of students had gathered around their chaperones. The air out here was somehow crisper than in town, even though it was the same wind that blew down from the peaks of the mountains. The sun was getting low in the sky, its glow a soft gold over the lodge and the big lawn behind. But the trees that surrounded them were already bathed in shadow. As Gracie gazed down the narrow path that led to the small wooden cabins where they would sleep, a crow cawed above them.

Gracie shivered, a chill going down her spine. She did *not* want to sleep in those dark woods in a cabin with people who made her uncomfortable.

"All right, folks, let's listen up!" Ms. Becker called over the sound of more than one hundred students talking and laughing. Most teachers would have to shout at least five more times, but Ms. Becker, the new seventh-grade English teacher, was so loved that pretty much everyone quieted right down.

"First a quick rundown of the most important rules," Ms. Becker began. "And remember, these are to keep everyone safe."

Gracie heard someone mutter "yeah, right" behind her as Ms. Becker quickly covered the curfew and the fact that no one could leave the cabins after lights out except with a teacher.

"The doors will be locked for your protection," Ms. Becker said, "but if you need a midnight pit stop, just wake up your chaperone—remember, that's what we're here for."

"To supervise us going to the bathroom?" Leo called out. Leo was always trying to be funny and generally failed. Still, he was basically harmless.

Most teachers would find his interruption annoying but Ms. Becker just laughed. The one thing Gracie had on her side was having Ms. Becker as chaperone.

"The entire campground is yours to explore, but always with a buddy and with one exception: We just got word that the cabin farthest from the lodge, Cobra, is being repaired, so that one's off-limits," Ms. Becker said. "That's also going to change our cabin assignments, so I'm going to read off the updated groups. As soon as you hear your name, take your stuff to your cabin. Dinner's in twenty minutes at the mess hall in the lodge, and I don't know about you, but nothing's going to keep me from those burgers and fries!"

Everyone cheered at that. Gracie did too—maybe with the new assignments, she'd be put with Mina!

"Sparrow Cabin is Mina, Nevaeh, Phoebe, and Hailey, supervised by the one and only Ms. Rivera," Ms. Becker called. So much for that, Gracie thought, her shoulders slumping.

Mina gave Gracie a quick hug, hoisted up her pack, and hurried to join her cabinmates.

Gracie felt like she'd swallowed an icicle as she watched Mina leave. Ms. Becker continued calling out assignments and Gracie's classmates hurried off in clusters. As the group dwindled down, Gracie saw Olivia off to one side, brushing her hair back absently, her expression serious. She wore leggings and a sweatshirt but still managed to look put together and stylish. Gracie, in sweatpants that were a bit snug around her tummy and a fleece hoodie, suddenly felt like a toddler.

She glanced around and found Jessica at the edge of the crowd, scrolling through her phone. All the seventh graders had been permitted to bring phones—parents had insisted—but they were off-limits except at specifically designated times. Still, half the class seemed to have their phones in their hands and the chaperones were apparently not going to make a thing of it. Gracie had heard a group of kids on the bus saying they'd snuck in laptops for gaming later, but Gracie had a feeling most of those would get confiscated. Only someone really crafty could conceal a laptop for a whole weekend.

"Okay, so the big change is to my group," Ms. Becker said, and Gracie turned to look back at her, not liking the tone that had crept into her normally cheery voice. "Mountain Lion is going to be coed."

Didn't that mean mixing boys and girls? Gracie looked at Ms. Becker, confused.

"With Cobra closed we have two boys without a place to sleep," the teacher went on. "So the new Mountain Lion crew, with me supervising, will be Olivia, Gracie, Leo, and Nicky."

Gracie drew in a breath as the icicle poked sharply into her chest. It was bad enough to have boys on the other side of the cabin wall, but *Nicky* was going to be one of them?

"Wait, what?" Olivia asked, putting a hand on her hip. "Isn't it against the rules for us to share like that?" She sounded flustered, which was very un-Olivia-like.

"It's fine," Ms. Becker said in a flat, firm voice that Gracie had never heard before. She and Olivia looked at each other for a moment and it was then that Gracie realized even Ms. Becker, a teacher, and a new one at that, knew what every seventh grader had known for years:

Nicky Finley was bad news. And no one wanted to be anywhere near him.

Snippet from the Snow Valley Police
Department Log
Missing Persons Case 3125
Time: 7:26 a.m.
Interview subject: Olivia Montgomery,
12 years old, accompanied by stepfather,
Jeremy Sutton
Cabinmate of Nicholas Finley

SERGEANT WILLIAMS:

You and Nicholas were in the same cabin, correct?

OLIVIA:

Yes, that's why I'm here, I think. Or are you inter-
viewing everyone?

SERGEANT WILLIAMS:

We are starting with those we know had contact
with Nicholas, yes.

OLIVIA:

I didn't have contact with him.

SERGEANT WILLIAMS:

So you didn't speak with him at all yesterday?

OLIVIA:

No.

SERGEANT WILLIAMS:

But you saw him in the cabin.

OLIVIA:

*I didn't look into the boys' side when I went in, so
no, I never saw him.*

SERGEANT WILLIAMS:

*What about at dinner or the campfire—did you see
him interacting with any of your classmates?*

OLIVIA:

*Nicky doesn't interact with people, he just—
actually, forget it. The answer is no, I didn't see him
interacting with anyone.*

SERGEANT WILLIAMS:

Not even his friends?

OLIVIA (SLIGHT LAUGH):

Nicky doesn't have friends.

CHAPTER 2

OLIVIA

Olivia threw her backpack onto the floor of bedroom one of the cabin with such force it bounced. She had hurried ahead of the others to avoid being near Nicky, though he hadn't been with the group in front of the lodge. He was probably off destroying flowers or menacing small animals in the woods. But still, Olivia did not want to be anywhere near him. She was livid that he had been put in her cabin.

"Is it okay if I come in?" Gracie asked timidly. She was standing in the doorway, biting on a cuticle, her curls falling over one cheek. Gracie was soft and sweet, which Olivia found pretty annoying. Yasmin had once called Gracie a bunny and it was a good description. Olivia herself was more like a mountain goat, pushing ahead no matter what. That was the only way to get what you wanted.

"Yeah, sorry, of course," Olivia said, gesturing for

her to enter the cozy room with its unfinished-wood floorboards and walls, bunk bed, and ladder. The one window looked out into the forest, and a pine-scented breeze gusted in. The room would have been perfect under other circumstances but now it felt claustrophobic and much, much too close to the boys' side. "Take either bunk. I don't care where I sleep."

Gracie seemed unnecessarily burdened by this. "Me neither," she said, a crease appearing between her brows as she looked warily at the bunk bed. "Um. You can choose."

Normally this would not have grated on Olivia, but normally she wasn't being forced to share a cabin with someone she hated. "Fine, I'll take the top," she said shortly, grabbing her pack and tossing it on the camp-issued sleeping bag that was spread neatly over the thin mattress.

Gracie's face was turning pink and she was blinking. Olivia had been too harsh.

"Sorry," Olivia said, trying to sound patient. Trying to *be* patient—it wasn't Gracie's fault Nicky was with them. And she had seen Gracie's expression when

Nicky's name was announced—she was upset too. "I'm just not happy with our cabin arrangements."

Gracie nodded and walked in the room to set her pack gently on the lower bunk.

"I hope that doesn't include me," a voice called from the front room. Olivia spun around, startled, to find Leo peeking his head in.

"It will if you sneak up on me like that again," Olivia informed him as she walked out of what was now officially the girls' room.

"Oh, I—" Leo began. Either he was anxious too or she had been harsh yet again.

"Just kidding," she said. "It's not you I care about." Then she caught herself. ". . . care about in a bad way, I mean."

Leo nodded and sighed. "At least you don't have to sleep in the same room as him."

This was a good point. "Yeah, that's rough," Olivia agreed.

"What happened to Jessica?" Gracie asked quietly. "Wasn't she supposed to be in this cabin?"

"I heard that she has such bad allergies that her

parents got the school to put her in a room in the lodge," Olivia said.

Gracie groaned.

"Seriously," Leo agreed. "I bet she doesn't even have allergies."

Olivia was irritated he'd say this with no knowledge of the situation—that was how false information was born. "She does, actually. Remember how she always used to sneeze when we went to the community garden back in elementary school? She has plant allergies and now she takes medication, but it probably doesn't last all night."

"Oh, I guess that makes sense," Leo said easily. Then he grinned. "I remember once she sneezed and shot snot all over Mr. Jenkins." He snorted happily at the memory and Olivia rolled her eyes.

Meanwhile, Gracie had been efficiently unpacking her things and getting her sleeping arranged on her bed. "I'm done. See you later," she said, so quietly Olivia almost missed it. Gracie hurried out, probably on her way to meet Mina, Olivia guessed. They were always together. Olivia would be that eager too, if *her* best friend were here.

"Hey, folks," Ms. Becker called as she opened the door to the cabin. She would be sleeping in the front room, which had a single bed and a little wooden table. There was a wall between the two bigger rooms, and both sides had to go through the front room to exit the cabin. "How's everyone doing?"

Olivia scowled. "I'm not happy about the new sleeping arrangements in our cabin." Leo looked surprised she was being that blunt, but Ms. Becker *had* asked.

Ms. Becker nodded for a moment. "I get that," she said. "It's a big change and changes can be hard." Her eyes told Olivia that she understood exactly what was so hard about this particular change. "But don't worry, we're going to have a great time."

Olivia couldn't help grinning at her teacher's enthusiasm. Leo was smiling too.

"Also, before I forget, I have to give you my cell phone number, in case you need to reach me for anything while we're here."

Leo looked confused. "But we can't use our phones except that half hour after meals."

"I think that you're going to be taking them on hikes and will be allowed to use them if there is an

21

emergency," Ms. Becker explained. "And if there is, call me."

She waited while Olivia and Leo got out their phones, then recited her number.

"Got it," Olivia said, tucking her phone into her backpack.

Someone opened the screen door of the cabin and Olivia stiffened, expecting Nicky, until she realized it was just Chloe, Ms. Becker's daughter, who was also in their grade.

"Hey," Olivia said.

Chloe nodded. Olivia hadn't spent much time with Chloe but she was nice enough, especially considering the fact that she'd had to move to a town where everyone had known one another forever. Being new in Snow Valley was not easy. It probably didn't help to see how popular her mom was either—and to have her mom teach in her grade.

"Hi," Chloe said, smiling shyly at Olivia.

"I'm glad you stopped by," Ms. Becker said to Chloe. "I'm waiting for Nicky but then we can go to dinner together, honey bee."

Chloe understandably winced. No one wanted to be called pet names by a parent in front of classmates.

So Olivia did the kind thing and headed out, Leo on her heels.

"It would be great to have a mom as cool as Ms. Becker," Leo said as they walked along the wood-chip path that wound through the trees.

Olivia could hear Coldwater Creek burbling behind the cabin. The creek started at the mountaintop and, after winding through the campground, flowed down to create Blackberry Pond outside town.

"Not if she was more popular than you," Olivia said, her feet crunching on a small pile of leaves. "Plus she's a mom—I'm sure she's annoying at home."

Leo kicked at one of the stones that lined the path, which irritated Olivia—someone had worked to put it there—but then he nodded. "You would know," he said bluntly.

Olivia laughed. "Yes, I definitely know." Her mom was probably the most popular lady in town because, along with Olivia's stepdad, she ran Exceptional People, an incredible comic book shop with a great candy selection and lots of places for customers to sit and read as long as they wanted. Plus the family dog, Sweet Thing, a tiny rescue that looked like a baby otter, snuggled in a doggy bed in the corner of the store all day. So yeah, Olivia's mom—and Jeremy—were as popular as grown-ups could be with the middle school crowd.

But as Olivia had said, at home they were just Mom and Jeremy, sometimes cool, sometimes crabby, and often annoying, especially about things like homework and screen time.

And lately they'd been a lot crabbier than usual.

The forest opened up to reveal the lodge and the big lawn surrounding it. The seventh grade had spread out over the picnic tables behind the two-story, log cabin–style building, and the smoky scent of sizzling meat made Olivia's stomach rumble.

"I'm going to eat at least four burgers," Leo boasted, like stuffing yourself was something impressive. Leo was always boasting about something stupid, which was what made him a pain. "The guys always say I can eat more than anyone."

"Have fun with that," Olivia said, turning to find her friends instead of heading inside to the mess hall to fill her plate. She was hungry but not hungry enough to wait in line with Leo.

She wove through tables of her classmates, who all seemed slightly different outside school somehow. Olivia always felt like this when they were on field trips, especially with teachers. Like now Mr. Patel had on a Mickey Mouse tee and gray hoodie instead of his usual school button-down shirt. It was both neat and weird.

"Hey," Angelica said when Olivia arrived. She and Ling had selected a table near the edge of the picnic area, and Olivia squinted against the brilliant colors of the sun sinking below the mountains in the distance, the pink so bright it was nearly neon. "Where's your food?"

"I was avoiding standing in line with Leo, but I'll go in now," Olivia said. She brushed back her bangs as she surveyed her friends. Ling wore hiking gear— her family went backpacking nearly every weekend so the woods were her second home. Angelica had on a My Pretty Pony sweatshirt over leggings. She loved silly things and could get away with wearing them. But unlike Olivia, she wore real hiking boots, not old Stan

Smiths, because she too hiked for real. She and Ling had been best friends since forever. Their group had the perfect balance when Yasmin went to Snow Valley Secondary, two sets of best friends hanging out as one fun crew. Olivia knew Angelica and Ling were always careful to include her now. But of course it wasn't the same.

"I thought it would be Nicky you were avoiding," Ling said, her usual friendly expression turning sour as she said his name. Olivia tensed up again at the thought of him. Yes, she would be avoiding Nicky at all costs.

Because Nicky was the reason Yasmin was gone.

Snippet from the Snow Valley Police Department Log

Missing Persons Case 3125

Time: 7:50 a.m.

Interview subject: Leo Harper-Jones, 12 years old, accompanied by mother, Isabelle Jones

Cabinmate of Nicholas Finley

SERGEANT WILLIAMS:

You and Nicholas shared a bunk bed, correct?

LEO:

Yeah, we did, but we didn't talk or anything. And I don't know what happened to him.

SERGEANT WILLIAMS:

Let's just take it one question at a time.

LEO:

Sure, okay, ah, yes, we shared a bunk bed. He was on the bottom. Wait, did you ask that?

SERGEANT WILLIAMS:

It's fine and there's no need to be nervous. I understand it's been an upsetting morning but you aren't in trouble. We're just doing our best to find

*Nicholas. You say you didn't speak at all? Not even
to discuss bunk selection?*

LEO:

*Right, yeah, most people probably did that, but I
just put my stuff on the floor when I came in and
then went to dinner. And after the campfire when I
got back, Nicky was already on the bottom bunk in
his sleeping bag.*

SERGEANT WILLIAMS:

Asleep?

LEO:

*I think so. I mean, probably, right? Why else would
he be in bed with his eyes closed?*

MS. JONES:

Leo, sweetie, relax, you're doing fine.

LEO:

Sorry, I never got questioned by a cop before.

SERGEANT WILLIAMS:

*Don't worry, just a few more questions. Did you
hear anything—anything at all—between the time
the lights went out last night and this morning,
when your chaperone discovered Nicholas was
missing?*

LEO:

Well, like, there were some noises outside. I heard an owl and then Mr. Windsor telling the kids in his cabin to be quiet.

SERGEANT WILLIAMS:

But it was quiet inside your cabin?

LEO:

Yeah, totally. It was really easy to fall asleep.

SERGEANT WILLIAMS:

This morning when you woke up—did anything seem out of place or unusual, besides the absence of Nicholas of course?

LEO:

. . .

SERGEANT WILLIAMS:

Leo?

LEO (CLEARS THROAT):

No, nothing unusual or out of place at all.

CHAPTER 3

LEO

"So did you bring it?" Steve asked, turning to Leo and cutting Gus off.

Gus had been boasting about his older brother Ben being the president of the high school tech club and the youngest kid to ever earn a green belt at the local karate school (ironic since Gus was terrible at tech and completely uncoordinated), but he fell silent now. Hunter and Alex, who had mostly been ignoring Leo up to this point, came to attention, and all of them pulled in a tight circle around Leo. They were so close that Leo could smell the fries from dinner on Steve's breath. Leo was already having trouble breathing because of the campfire smoke blowing in their faces, and he coughed slightly.

"Yeah, of course I did," Leo said, trying to come off as nonchalant. But his voice was constricted from the smoke and it was hard to sound nonchalant when he was zipping with nerves, as his Grandma Bethany would say.

"Where is it?" Gus asked eagerly, like Leo was just going to present it right there, at the campfire with all their classmates and teachers surrounding them.

"It's in my stuff, at the cabin," Leo said. The fire gave a loud crackle and Leo flinched. He was zipping with nerves for sure, but luckily no one noticed.

"Duh, obviously," Steve said to Gus, who cowered. Leo felt the usual flush of relief that someone other than him was the target of Steve's scorn. He felt bad for Gus too, of course, but Gus and the others had all made the hockey team, while Leo had not. So the usual target of scorn was Leo. When they bothered talking to him anyway. He and the guys had been tight since playing on the Pucksters, the Snow Valley hockey league for elementary school kids, but while the other four had gotten so good they made starters on the school team as seventh graders, Leo had stayed pretty much the same. And he had not made the team, even as a benchwarmer. He blamed his parents for this—while the other guys had normal, hockey-obsessed parents (why else live in hockey country?), Mom was all about yoga and Dad took power walks, which was mortifying. Then there was his little sister, Helena, who insisted on wearing a tutu everywhere and dancing instead of walking at the grocery store. The only cool one in the family was his older brother, Noah, who was so good at rock climbing he'd been written up in the paper. Noah probably would have driven Leo to hockey workshops and camps if he could—Leo had lucked out when it came to brothers, which was why he felt so guilty about what he'd done this afternoon. But Noah was only fifteen and Mom and Dad called hockey extras a waste of money. They didn't get that hockey was what boys in Snow Valley *did*. As a result of this failure, Leo was now a near outcast with his friends and had to resort to desperate measures to stay part of the group.

But on the bright side the measures had worked because Steve was grinning at Leo like Leo had just scored the winning goal. And the other guys, as always, were following his lead. "Very cool," Steve said. "You'll show us tomorrow."

It was not a question but Leo still bobbed his head. "Yup, for sure. I'm psyched about it."

This could not have been less true.

Steve held up his hand and Leo gave him a high five. It almost made the lie—and all Leo had done this afternoon—worth it.

"All right, folks, that's a wrap!" Mr. Patel called over the noise of 108 seventh graders set loose in the wild. "You have five minutes to get back to your cabins for a head count. Sleep well tonight because that ropes course tomorrow is waiting and it is for real."

Leo joined in the cheers despite the fact that he had a fear of heights. The ropes course, which was mostly in treetops, was his worst nightmare. But Steve and the others were whooping, so Leo clapped and then pumped a fist. If the guys were into it, Leo was into it.

"See you tomorrow, dude," Steve said to Leo, thumping his shoulder.

A warmth flooded through Leo at Steve's words and his look of admiration. Yes, what Leo had done was worth it. He was grinning the whole way back to Mountain Lion, despite the fact that it was very dark and actual mountain lions may have been lurking.

The restrooms were right near his cabin, so Leo made a quick stop. After washing his hands, he hesitantly opened the screen door, stepping slowly out of the dimly lit bathroom into the dark woods. A sliver of moonlight cast an eerie glow on the trees above Leo, surrounding him with inky shadows. Just then there came a sharp crackling sound, and a small screech slipped through Leo's lips.

"Relax, wimp," Gus huffed, his voice floating through the darkness from the path. "It's just me."

"Yeah, no big deal," Leo said, trying to keep his voice low to regain some of his dignity.

Gus rolled his eyes and shook his head as he continued back toward his cabin, Wolf, which was on the opposite side of the campground.

"Did you have fun tonight?" Ms. Becker asked when Leo walked into the cabin, which was lit by lanterns that glowed softly in each of the rooms. She had already changed into flannel PJs, which made Leo instantly embarrassed. Teachers were not supposed to wear PJs. Plus what if there was some kind of emergency? She was hardly dressed to save them from a fire or animal attack.

"Yeah, it was good," Leo mumbled, hurrying to his side of the cabin despite the fact he wasn't looking forward to being there with Nicky, who was extremely unpleasant to everyone. Leo had never had a run-in with him, thankfully, but last year Steve had mocked Nicky's jeans, which were too short, and Nicky had retaliated by spray-painting Steve's hockey gear. Not that anyone could prove it was Nicky—Nicky never got caught for the stuff he did. But he made sure Steve knew who was responsible and ever since then all the guys stayed clear of him. Especially Leo, which was why this cabin pairing was so unfortunate.

But then Leo saw that Nicky was already in his sleeping bag, pillow over his head, facing the wall. He had a large, ratty red backpack at the foot of the bed, with a pair of rubber fishing boots next to it. That seemed weird—there was no fishing on the trip. But whatever, what mattered was that he was asleep and Leo wouldn't have to deal with him today. Leo breathed a small sigh of relief as he tiptoed over to where he'd left his own backpack at the foot of the bed. It wasn't there, and for a moment he felt a rush of panic, but then he glanced around the room and saw it was leaning against the wall in the corner. Had Nicky moved it? Maybe it had been in his way. Leo was about to open the bag when the floorboards creaked, making him jump a mile.

"Sorry, hon, didn't mean to scare you," Ms. Becker said quietly. "Just wanted to see if you need to brush your teeth or use the facilities—remember it's lights out so if nature calls, be sure to wake me up to walk you to the restrooms."

Leo just shook his head vigorously and climbed quickly into his bunk.

"I'm good, thanks," he said, momentarily getting tangled in the sleeping bag. Normally he did like to brush his teeth at night—otherwise they felt mossy in the morning—but he obviously couldn't start digging around in his bag with Ms. Becker right there.

"Sleep well," Ms. Becker said, leaning over to turn off the lantern. The room was dark, with shadows flitting in from the light still shining on the other side. Leo heard one of the girls come in and chat briefly with Ms. Becker. A few minutes later, the lights were all out and the cabin was dark. Leo breathed in a deep breath of the mountain air blowing gently through the window.

He fell asleep smiling, knowing that tomorrow with the guys would be epic. Totally and completely epic.

PART 2

CHAPTER 4

GRACIE

"Okay, everybody on," Coach Tiffins called. The seventh grade had been huddled in front of the lodge for the past ten minutes, waiting for the buses to arrive.

Gracie shakily made her way up the stairs and into the humid bus as the coach asked them all to keep quiet and board calmly.

After discovering that Nicky was missing, teachers had called the police, and the police had asked them to "vacate the cabins promptly" so they could do a thorough investigation of each one. So now they were headed down the driveway, the same one they had thumped their way up the afternoon before. The potholes were the same but everything—*everything*—else was different. An eerie quiet pervaded the bus. People kept glancing back at Gracie sitting snug next to Mina, whose arm was tight around her.

But Gracie was still chilled to the core.

41

"So you woke up and he was gone?" Mina whispered.

"Not exactly," Gracie said, closing her eyes and trying not to remember being jarred from a deep sleep by Ms. Becker yelling if anyone had seen Nicky. The teacher's voice had been shrill and shaky, and Gracie was instantly terrified. And that was before Ms. Becker burst into their room, her eyes wild in spite of the fact she was clearly trying to keep it together. "Ms. Becker woke me—and Olivia and I think Leo too—she was shouting about Nicky because she'd realized he was gone."

"That must have been scary," Mina said, giving Gracie a squeeze.

Gracie nodded. "Yeah, she couldn't hide the fact she was totally freaked out. I've never seen a teacher like that. But she'd already checked with the campground staff and the other chaperones, so she knew it was bad."

Eric Kepner, who was sitting in front of them, turned around, resting his hands on the seat back. "What was it like talking to the cops?"

"Mind your own business," Mina snapped. "And leave Gracie alone."

But just the mention of the police had Gracie

closing her eyes again, trying to escape this nightmare situation. The cops had been there by the time the three of them left the cabin, and she, Olivia, and Leo were immediately brought to the lodge, where a makeshift interview room was set up. Gracie's mom had gotten there first so they went in before Olivia or Leo. Icy sweat had slithered down her sides as she answered their questions, and she'd picked her cuticles on her thumb and forefinger so badly they'd bled. Afterward, Gracie had gone to grab a tissue at the front desk when she'd overheard two cops discussing—

She shook her head, trying to toss off the scary memory. She felt sick to her stomach.

"I'm glad your mom let you ride back on the bus," Mina said.

Gracie nodded. She'd begged her mom to let her stay with Mina and take the bus back to town, where her mom would meet her in the school parking lot. But her relief was more than just the comfort of being with her friend. Mom, who was a therapist, would have known something was eating at Gracie, something more than a missing classmate and a chat with the police. And she couldn't handle that right now.

"Do you want to come over? We can bake cookies and watch movies," Mina asked, reading Gracie's mind as she often did. "We can watch anything you want." Mina was a big movie snob so this was a very generous offer. "I think your mom will let you if you tell her it's what you need."

Mom probably would—being a therapist made her especially good at listening to Gracie and respecting what she said. But Gracie was concerned she might peel off her skin if all she did this afternoon was watch movies. Or go home. She needed to *do* something. But what?

Eric's head popped up over the seat back again, his eyes big. "I heard the cops think Nicky was kidnapped! Did they—"

"Back off!" Mina shouted so fiercely the whole bus froze. "No one talks to Gracie," she went on, turning so that everyone experienced her harsh gaze. "No questions, no comments, nothing. Got it?"

Coach Tiffins, the only chaperone on their bus (Ms. Becker was still working with the police back at the campsite), stood up. "You heard her," he yelled. "And no more yelling on the bus."

Coach Tiffins often made very little sense but Gracie was glad he hadn't been mad at Mina.

"Jeez," Eric muttered, but he slouched back around and Gracie had the feeling he wouldn't be speaking to her again for a while.

"Thanks," she said to Mina, who nodded reassuringly. Generally Mina was easygoing but certain things, like someone giving a person she cared about a hard time, brought out her protective side. Gracie did not have a side like this so she was very grateful for Mina's. Mina, like Mom, assumed Gracie was traumatized by waking up in a cabin with a classmate missing. Which she was, of course. But the real trauma, the thing that was biting into Gracie's intestines, scraping the insides of her lungs, and squeezing her throat, was so awful Gracie could not bear to share it with her friends or even Mom. Eric was right—the police did believe Nicky had been kidnapped—Gracie had heard them say so when she was getting the tissue for her bloody fingers. They said Nicky "fit the profile of a familial kidnapping," words that had made Gracie's insides tangle up like a nest of baby snakes. Because if that was true and if anyone found out what Gracie had done—

Gracie clamped down on these thoughts, promising herself that Nicky would be found quickly and that he would be fine. As long as that happened, no one would ever need to know Gracie's toxic truth.

The bus had left the forest behind and was passing by Lane Sanctuary, where Gracie's family had adopted Puffin, their super friendly bunny. Gracie wished Puffin were on the bus with her now—his soft, warm weight in her lap was always extremely soothing. They coasted down Winding Valley Road, which twined from the peaks outside town down to the valley. It was the hub of most hiking trails, including Kappa Path, which led from town to the campground they'd just left. Gracie turned her head to avoid seeing it and instead looked at the big weathered homes, most with hardy flower bushes and plants that could survive a cold mountain winter.

A few minutes later the bus had turned into the parking lot of Snow Valley Secondary, the large brick building that housed both the middle and high schools. The lot was full of cars parked haphazardly: the families of the seventh graders coming to collect their kids after the disaster of a class trip. The driver pulled to a stop at the usual bus drop-off lane, though nothing about this drop-off was usual. Gracie pulled her pack over her shoulder as she and her classmates filed into the aisle. This time there was no pushing and barely a word spoken. And of course no Nicky in the back being obnoxious.

Coach Tiffins stood at the bus exit, directing students to stand in a line and wait for their family members to collect them, something that hadn't happened since they'd graduated from elementary school two years earlier. Eric was rolling his eyes but Gracie had to admit it was comforting not to have to fight the crowd to find Mom.

"Coach!" a woman shouted loudly, and Gracie noticed Eric wince.

"Yes," Coach shouted back as he looked up from his phone, confused, then grimaced. "Hello there, Mrs. Kepner."

Gracie knew Eric's mom had a reputation for giving teachers a hard time—she was kind of infamous for it.

"Do we need to keep our kids inside because a kidnapper is on the loose?" she asked, grabbing Eric, who was turning red, by the shoulder.

"Well, I'm not really sure . . ." Coach Tiffins trailed off, looking around and then waving rather frantically at Ms. Rivera, who walked over. Gracie saw that she had circles under her eyes and her face seemed creased with worry.

"No," Ms. Rivera said when Mrs. Kepner repeated her question. "Principal Montenegro sent out a direct message from the police stating that no other children are in danger at this time."

"Are they certain?" Mrs. Kepner asked, pulling Eric closer. He tried to squirm away but his mother's grip was ferocious.

"Yes," Ms. Rivera said reassuringly. "They were very clear that there is nothing to suggest an active kidnapper is roaming the area."

Mrs. Kepner nodded tightly. "Thank you," she said, then hauled Eric off. It was clear that no matter what the teachers said, Eric was going to be staying inside until Nicky was home safe.

Gracie heard a few of her classmates snicker but she was too anxious to care that Eric had been embarrassed. Because while it was great no one else was in danger, the police thought Nicky had been kidnapped by a family member. And if he had—

Gracie leaned back against the bus, not caring that it was probably dirty, and closed her eyes. Heavy exhaust fumes in the air, along with the worry in her belly, were starting to make her head ache.

"Gracie."

Gracie opened her eyes and saw a very agitated Olivia standing in front of her.

"We need to talk, now," Olivia said, grabbing Gracie's wrist.

Mina glared at Olivia. "Only if Gracie feels like it."

Olivia's gaze bored into Gracie, who nodded. "Okay," she said, allowing Olivia to pull her away from her classmates. Coach Tiffins was on his phone, probably checking sports scores, and didn't see them duck around the back of the bus, where Gracie was surprised to see Leo waiting. He waved like everything was normal.

"I need your help," Olivia announced.

This was the last thing Gracie had expected her to say. "Really?"

"Yes," Olivia said, rapidly shifting her weight from leg to leg, which was making Gracie's stress level rise. Olivia was really worked up. "Tell me everything you guys remember from the cabin last night and this morning."

"Um, what?" Gracie asked. Her brain was clogged with anxiety, and this request was both overwhelming and nonsensical.

"I have to figure out what happened to Nicky and I need to figure it out ASAP," Olivia said, the words coming out so fast they piled into one another. "There have to be clues in the cabin that the police aren't noticing, but I can't think of anything. I need to know what you and Leo remember. I need you to help me—"

"—brainstorm," Leo said.

Olivia nodded. "Yeah. Share anything you can think of. Maybe something you saw will get me to remember more and hopefully lead to the clues that will help me find Nicky."

"I'm not sure we can find clues left by a kidnapper," Gracie began, queasy from stress. "Don't they cover their tracks well?"

"I don't believe for a second that he was kid-napped," Olivia said shortly.

"Really?" Gracie asked again, this time with hope. If Nicky *hadn't* been kidnapped, everything would be okay . . .

"Really," Olivia said, her voice hard. "I know for a fact that Nicky was finally getting payback for all the horror he's unleashed." In this moment Gracie could tell Olivia read a lot of comics because who else would say something like "the horror he's unleashed"? Gracie kind of liked it. "He's hiding."

"He's gone dark," Leo said knowingly.

"Yeah, he has to have gone dark," Olivia said, rais-ing a brow and nodding in a satisfied way.

Cars continued to pull out of the lot as families picked up their kids and the fumes were now making Gracie's head pound. Plus she knew Mom was waiting and she needed to go back to the line. But first she had to find out what Olivia was talking about.

"What do you mean Nicky was 'getting payback'?" she asked.

Olivia brushed this off. "It's a long story and I can't

get into it—the clock is ticking and I have to find Nicky. But trust me, I know what he's trying to hide from."

This was both mysterious and frustrating because how could Gracie know for sure Olivia was right and Nicky was hiding unless she knew the whole story? She tugged on a lock of hair so hard it hurt.

"I'm in," Leo said.

Olivia's brows scrunched. "What do you mean?"

"I'll help brainstorm but after that I'm not just going home—I'm going with you," Leo said, his expression tense as he spoke. "I have my own reason for needing to find Nicky."

"What is it?" Olivia asked, tilting her head, clearly intrigued.

"It's a long story and I can't get into it," Leo said, smirking slightly. "But I'm searching for Nicky too."

Olivia shrugged. "Sure, as long as you don't get in my way and as long as you tell me everything you remember—every taste, smell, and thing you saw."

This seemed over-the-top to Gracie but Leo nodded.

"Gracie, can you help us before you go home?" Olivia asked. "Just tell us anything that stuck out as odd."

Gracie gulped because she was about to say

something she did not want to say. But what choice did she have? She *had* to find out what had happened to Nicky. "No."

"What?" Olivia asked, her eyes widening in shock.

"I mean no, I won't tell you what I remember and then go home either," Gracie said. Her voice was shrill in her ears. "I'll brainstorm but I'm in too, just like Leo. I'm going to help you guys find Nicky."

CHAPTER 5

OLIVIA

When Olivia pulled up on her bike, she saw Leo was already at the bench in front of the polar bear statue in the town square. She ducked to avoid being in the photo two tourists were taking in front of the statue. There were obviously no polar bears in the Catskill Mountains, but tourists loved the statue and that was the point. Snow Valley survived on tourism and while some things, like restaurants none of the locals could afford, were obnoxious, the statue was cute. Olivia's little brother, Benji, always insisted they visit the bear first thing whenever the family came into town.

Leo's bike was tossed on the ground behind the bench, but she stood hers next to the statue and carefully lowered the kickstand before taking off her helmet.

"Hey, Liv," Gemma, a ninth grader who had lived next door to Yasmin, called as she walked past with her friend Ally, who also waved. Ally's family ran Lane Animal Sanctuary, where over half the town, including Olivia's family, had adopted rescue pets.

Olivia waved and glanced around for Gracie as she headed to Leo. Olivia had been shocked when Gracie announced she wanted to help track down Nicky. Gracie was not a bold detective; she was a meek rule follower and never did anything without Mina. Even if she did show up, Olivia didn't think she'd stick it out for long. Whatever happened, though, Olivia would not stop until Nicky had been found.

The square was surrounded by the town hall, the post office, the police department, and Maple Street, the main stretch of touristy stores and restaurants. (Practical things like the grocery and hardware store were a few blocks away on Oak Drive). It was dotted with trees, flower beds, and several other statues, as well as benches, and was a popular hangout spot for tourists and locals alike.

"So what's the story?" Leo asked, rubbing his forehead as Olivia came over to him. "What's the payback coming to Nicky?"

As Olivia thought about how to answer him, she

spotted Gracie crossing Maple to walk her bike down one of the narrow paths to meet them.

Olivia gritted her teeth for a moment because there wasn't time to waste talking about this. But Leo and Gracie *were* helping, at least for the moment, so they deserved to know—plus they'd see how urgent it was that they locate Nicky.

"Okay," Olivia began as Gracie approached them. "Here's the deal. Remember how Nicky had a big argument with that eighth grader Ryan where Ryan accused Nicky of stealing his lunch card?"

"Nicky did steal it," Leo said, indignant. "Ryan sits at my lunch table with the other hockey guys and he told us he got in a lot of trouble because his parents thought he was just careless and lost it."

As far as Olivia knew, Leo was not a hockey guy himself—she'd never seen him at games or practices—but the hockey guys did mostly all sit together at three big central tables where there would be room for a non-hockey guy like Leo to join them.

"I bet," Olivia said, getting back on track. "And then remember two days later there was that 'glitch'"—she made air quotes—"in the school computer and Ryan's failing math grade got posted on the school website and everyone saw it?" Olivia raised her eyebrows. There was nothing glitchy about what had happened.

Gracie was nodding her head as she looped her helmet over her handlebars. "We all knew that was Nicky—he's the only one who can hack into the school computer—or at least he could before all that drama in Clarksdale and the new firewall." She sat on the bench next to Leo, looking at Olivia intently.

Leo nodded grimly. "It was lucky for us that Clarksdale happened or who knows what else Nicky would have done with that skill set."

Clarksdale Middle School, about an hour north of them, had suffered a huge hack, with nearly half the sixth grade getting their grades changed. It had been particularly bad because teachers' grade books were online and they got hacked too. The whole thing had been in the news, and when it came out that a student was responsible, the state Department of Education had invested in major firewall protection to avoid being embarrassed again. Which had been a relief to everyone in Snow Valley.

"Anyway, Ryan's still angry," Olivia went on. She

shifted her weight from one foot to the other as she spoke. She found it soothed her to move when she talked about something stressful. "Obviously—who wouldn't be? His card was stolen and then he got humiliated for trying to get it back. So he's been planning payback: He's been talking to everyone Nicky's bullied or harassed and taking down their stories, all the details and evidence. He called Yasmin last week—that's how I know about it. Ryan figures with this many people reporting on the same person and giving details and stuff, Principal Montenegro will have to believe them and look into it. But then—"

"Ohhhh!" Leo exclaimed, bouncing a little on the bench. "Nicky found out about the list?"

"That's why he disappeared. To figure out some way to stop it from ever coming out," Olivia confirmed, nodding.

"But how can he stop it?" Gracie asked. Wrapped in a raspberry-colored fleece, she did look as fuzzy and uncertain as a bunny.

"No idea, but that's the thing," Olivia said. "If we let him have enough time, he'll come up with something. He always does." Her voice curdled.

Leo was looking at her, one brow slightly raised. "Why are *you* so invested in him getting in trouble for everything? Did he do something to you?"

Olivia pressed her lips together as hot flames licked her insides. "He made Yasmin so miserable her family had to move," she said shortly.

Leo let out a loud sigh and shook his head.

"So, yeah, I need to see him punished for ruining my best friend's life," Olivia said, biting off each word. "And that's why I'm finding whatever hole he's hiding in and making sure he sees justice."

"*We're* finding him," Leo corrected.

"Right," Olivia said. She felt briefly curious what made Leo so fervent about tracking down Nicky. Why would he care, if Nicky had never done anything to him? But she didn't have time to get into it. Whatever it was, it clearly had him motivated, and that was all that mattered.

"Okay, it's time to get started," she announced. "Let me just grab us some fuel."

She hustled over to her bike and reached into the basket for a bag of chips she'd picked up along the way.

"My parents give me money for junk food, so I bought us these," she said, carrying them over. "We're going to need energy for this."

"They seriously give you money for chips?" Leo asked, once again shocked. "I think my parents would pay me to *not* eat junk food."

Olivia laughed as she passed Leo the bag. He tore it open immediately, causing a delicious puff of barbecue dust to perfume the air.

"Yeah, my brother Benji's autistic and he's really particular about food right now. My parents don't want me to feel restricted by his choices so I get a junk food allowance." Benji was fussy about the texture of food and often decided he would only eat certain colors, so to make sure Olivia wasn't impacted, Mom and Jeremy gave her money every week for her own snacks. Which obviously meant junk food.

"That is very cool," Leo said, reaching into the bag for a handful of chips.

Olivia nodded, scooping up her own handful. Mom had done a lot of reading on autism, and part of that included making sure siblings like Olivia were not "negatively impacted by household changes."

If only it were so easy to do something about what truly negatively impacted her about her brother's diagnosis.

Olivia focused back on Gracie and Leo. "Okay, so let's go over the night we spent in the cabin. What do you guys remember? What did you see? We're looking for anything out of the ordinary—anything that can give us a clue as to where Nicky went."

Leo's mouth was stuffed with chips—clearly it had been a mistake to hand him the bag—but after a moment Gracie spoke up. "I didn't really look in their room closely, but I did see one thing I thought was weird: Nicky brought waders but we weren't going fishing. Unless those were yours, Leo?"

"No," Leo said, his words muffled by chips. "I saw those too and they definitely seemed off. The packing list said to bring hiking boots if we had them, not rubber boots."

"Interesting," Olivia mused.

"And here's the other thing," Leo said, brushing off his mouth, which was covered in red barbecue powder. "They were gone this morning. Wherever he went, he wore the boots and left his sneakers behind."

"*Very* interesting," Olivia said. "What do you guys think it means?"

There was silence except for the crinkling of the bag as Leo shoveled more chips into his mouth. Gracie had helped herself to one single chip and was now carefully brushing off her fingers.

Olivia sighed and reached over to grab some chips for herself. "Okay, we can come back to the boots later. Anything else?"

"Did he take his backpack, or was that left behind in the cabin too?" Gracie asked Leo softly. The wind was picking up and her curls blew gently over her shoulders.

"No, he took it. The only thing he left was his sneakers," Leo said. He waved at someone and Olivia turned to see a couple of hockey guys, Steve and Gus, with skate bags and sticks over their shoulders. Gus, who had been looking intently at Leo, gave her a quick mock salute.

"When you got to the bunk, could you see what he had in his backpack?" Gracie asked.

Olivia was impressed with Gracie's questions—they were smart.

Leo chewed and contemplated for a moment. "I could tell he had his computer—the corner of it stuck out through a gap in the zipper. I couldn't see anything else inside though." He paused and burped loudly.

"So super gross," Olivia informed Leo, annoyed. Gracie was sliding away from Leo on the bench—the burp had probably smelled as gross as it sounded.

"This was strange though," Leo said, clearly getting excited as he remembered something. "His backpack was big and it was really full. Like he'd stuffed it with a bunch of things."

Olivia nodded in satisfaction. Now they were getting somewhere. "Right. Like I said—because he planned to run away so he needed supplies."

"But we don't know for sure he ran away," Gracie said. The sharpness of her tone surprised Olivia.

"Sure he did," she said. "What else could have happened?"

"He could have been kidnapped by a family member," Gracie said, clearly agitated. "That's what the police think and they're experts."

Olivia brushed this away. "They don't know Nicky like we do," she said. "So they're just wrong."

Gracie did not look convinced. For a moment Olivia wondered why meek Gracie cared so much about finding Nicky—he hadn't done anything to her, at least not that Olivia knew of, and Olivia knew most of the awful things Nicky had done.

"I agree," Leo said, this time spraying chips.

Olivia snatched the chips bag from him. "No more for you—my little brother eats more neatly."

"Probably because he doesn't get enough junk food," Leo sulked, reaching out one foot to scuff a small pile of leaves.

"Okay, do we remember anything else?" Olivia asked, biting back her smile, because that had been kind of funny—but Leo didn't need to know she thought so.

There was silence again and then Gracie spoke up. "I don't . . . but there was someone else in the cabin we could ask—if we can figure out how to get in touch with her."

"Ms. Becker!" Olivia cried. She had not thought to ask the teacher. It was a great idea!

"We just have to find out her number or address,"

Gracie said again. "Though maybe it's rude to knock on her door?"

Olivia already had her phone out and was scrolling through her contacts to get to the one most recently added.

"That won't be necessary," she told Gracie, pushing on the call icon on her phone once she had located her teacher. "I've got it right here. Let's see what Ms. Becker has to say."

CHAPTER 6

LEO

Leo watched as Olivia strode to the other side of the polar bear statue, phone pressed to her ear. He didn't share her confidence that the teacher would be willing to talk about this but it was worth a try. And he was still hungry, so while they waited he grabbed the bag of chips Olivia had left on the bench. After stuffing a handful in his mouth, he held it out to Gracie.

"No, thanks," she said, turning her head slightly away.

"Not into barbecue?" Leo asked, the words muffled by chips. It was possible his manners weren't the best right now, but he was starving after missing breakfast at the campground because he was with the police. And then rushing home only to grab his bike so he could meet Olivia and Gracie ASAP. Nothing mattered more than finding Nicky, but having a snack was pretty nice.

Gracie grimaced slightly. "This is going to sound strange," she said, her voice soft, "but I have a really good sense of smell—like, too good. When I was a little kid, I couldn't walk by a garbage can without retching."

"Did you ever puke out on the street?" Leo asked, very interested in this topic. Plus it was a good distraction while they waited for Olivia.

Gracie scrunched her nose and nodded.

"Do you still puke when you walk by garbage cans?" Leo asked. This was so cool! Super gross but very cool.

"No, it's a lot better now," Gracie said, which was disappointing. "But strong smells like barbecue bother me."

Leo nodded, shoving more chips in his mouth. A group of high schoolers had arrived and were tossing a Frisbee a little too close by for Leo's comfort. On a windy day the breeze could snatch a Frisbee and turn it into a weapon, something Leo knew a lot about. Last summer when he'd been playing Frisbee with the guys, he'd been distracted by a bee and gotten whaled in the back of the head. Steve and the others made fun of him for weeks, which he got—it had been a pretty weak moment. But the bump on his head had taken over a month to heal and Leo did not want to experience that again.

"Olivia is really determined to find Nicky," Gracie said, glancing over to where Olivia stood under one of the big orange-gold-and-green-leafed oak trees.

Leo looked too and saw that Olivia was nodding intently. "Yeah, she's ruthless about it," he said.

"Ruthless?" Gracie's forehead was wrinkling. Leo had never spent time with her outside the occasional group work and it was becoming obvious she was very sensitive—she reminded him of his seven-year-old sister, Helena, who his mom said "felt things deeply," which didn't make a ton of sense because didn't everyone? But Helena *was* always getting worked up about something.

"Ruthless in a good way," Leo reassured her. "We need to find Nicky." Leo did not want to even consider the possibility that they could fail. Because if they didn't find Nicky before the sun went down (which was the time Leo had to be back home), he was in the kind of trouble nightmares were made of.

Gracie nodded with a surprising amount of vigor as Olivia came up, shoulders slumped and face pinched.

"Ms. Becker wouldn't tell you anything?" Leo asked, sliding over to make room on the bench.

"Worse," Olivia said, flopping down next to him. "She wouldn't even speak to me. Chloe answered her mom's phone and she'd obviously been crying. She said her mom got put on leave."

"Wait, *what*?" Gracie asked, grabbing Leo's arm and digging her fingers in so hard he yelped. Which was the kind of thing Steve would mock him for, but Gracie just dropped his arm with a quick "Sorry."

"Ms. Becker was our chaperone," Olivia said, looking evenly at Gracie, clearly taken aback by her harsh reaction too. And Olivia wasn't even going to have the bruises Leo knew were coming to him. *What* was up with Gracie? "She was the teacher in charge and Nicky went missing on her watch. So yeah, unless he's found soon with a really good reason for disappearing, she's in trouble."

"Could she go to prison?"

Both Olivia and Leo jumped at Gracie's loud, high-pitched question, and a robin that had been perched on the statue flew away.

"I don't think so," Olivia said, casting a glance at Leo. "I meant she could be in trouble for her job—she might get fired."

That was awful but of course it also made sense— Leo knew teachers were responsible for kids in all kinds of ways, and one disappearing when you were supposed to be keeping them safe was not good.

Gracie bent forward, resting her face against her knees.

"Gracie, are you okay?" Olivia asked. She sounded both concerned and impatient as she stood up from the bench.

"Yeah," Gracie said, her voice muffled. "I just need a second."

"I get that," Leo said, giving Olivia a look. "We all love Ms. Becker." To be honest, he didn't completely get why Gracie's reaction was so extreme but he knew from experience to give someone space when they needed it—Helena had taught him well.

"Just *one* second though," Olivia said firmly, brushing her bangs to the side. She was shifting her weight back and forth, something Leo found distracting. "The clock is ticking."

Leo bit back a retort because he definitely didn't feel like tangling with Olivia. And in fairness, he too wanted to get things moving with the search for Nicky. "So what's our next move?" he asked. "In comics they talk to someone's friends to see where the suspect might have hidden. But Nicky doesn't have any friends so that's out."

Olivia snorted. "Truth. Yeah, I think in Nicky's case we have to talk to his enemies, and that means talking to Ryan since not only is he Nicky's enemy, he's talked to everyone else who's mad at Nicky too."

Leo nodded—it was a smart next move. He didn't know Ryan well—in the cafeteria the actual hockey players sat in the center seats while Leo hung on at the end of the far bench. But from the little he'd seen, Ryan was a nice guy.

"Gracie, are you ready?" Olivia asked.

Gracie lifted her head. Her eyes were watery and her normally pink cheeks were pale, but she nodded.

"Let's go," Olivia said, clapping her hands as if she were a teacher rushing them to get their notebooks out.

"Okay," Leo said, standing as a sudden breeze blew the chips bag out of his hands. "I just—"

Olivia snatched the bag as it flew by her and then glared at Leo. "You finished them."

"Yeah, and I'm dying for something to drink," he said. His throat had never been drier. "Let's stop at—"

"Too bad, we're in a rush," Olivia interrupted, marching to the garbage can.

Leo glanced curiously at Gracie, who was right behind Olivia, but she showed no signs of puking. "It'll just take three seconds," he said. "It's not like we even know where Ryan lives—at least I don't. It'll take more than three seconds to find out. You guys can do that while I grab a soda."

"Yasmin told me he has an office at the library," Olivia said, striding toward Maple Street and nearly plowing into a kid on a scooter. "He works there or at the benches outside."

"He has an office?" Leo asked, confused. How did you get an office at the library? Leo loved the library, and now he wanted an office there too.

"I think she means metaphorically," Gracie said to him as they hustled to keep up with Olivia. Gracie's face was still a bit pasty but she had a look of determination that Leo appreciated. "Like that's where he's been meeting with everyone to collect the evidence against Nicky and stuff."

"Oh, that makes more sense," Leo said, once again disappointed. Then he glanced at Gracie, who was struggling to put her long hair back in a ponytail so it would stop blowing in her face. She wasn't doing that well and Leo was surprised the hair wasn't choking her—she had so much of it. "Listen, can you back me up on the drink thing?" he asked quietly, then nearly slipped on a pile of leaves he hadn't noticed in the path. This was what happened when he got too thirsty—the rest of him stopped working. And he had to be working to help find Nicky.

Gracie's forehead once again crinkled. "I don't want her to get mad at me," she whispered.

"She won't," Leo said confidently, regaining his balance. "She's nice to you."

"Actually she almost took my head off in the cabin yesterday," Gracie said, finally wrestling most of her hair into the rubber band.

"I did not," Olivia said, whirling around.

Both Gracie and Leo jumped back.

"I just wanted you to choose the bunk," Olivia said,

hands on her hips. "And Leo, we can get your stupid drink but it better be fast."

"Great," Leo said, relieved. "Let's go to—"

"We're going to the Corner Store," Olivia roared. "Because it's on the way to the library." Then she grinned. "That's what it looks like when I take your head off."

Gracie was blinking rapidly. Leo was starting to worry she wouldn't make it through a full day with Olivia, though she did seem committed. He wondered again: Why was she so determined to help apprehend Nicky? What had he done to her? It must have been bad to make someone so seemingly fragile stick with the quest. But Nicky *had* done some pretty awful stuff. Like the incident last spring when for reasons unknown (or nonexistent) Nicky had embedded a piece of gum in Jessica Potter's hair so thoroughly that she had to cut off a big chunk of it, giving her a bald spot that briefly earned her the nickname Naked Mole Rat. Luckily for her, the name had been too long to stick, and she'd immediately started spending all her free time in the tech center to avoid everyone—understandable as far as Leo was concerned.

They reached the crosswalk just as the light changed and headed to the other side of the street. Moments later Olivia was pushing open the door to the Corner Store. The shop sold a wide array of drinks, candy, and junk food, as well as newspapers, stationery products, and postcards of Snow Valley. Mr. Rodriguez, the longtime owner, stood behind the counter, and he beamed when he saw them.

"Hello to three of my favorite people!" he said. He said this to everyone, but Leo was convinced he meant it—Mr. Rodriguez was always excited to see whoever walked through the door, whether they bought anything or not. Which was probably why so many people came to his store when they needed pretzels or a new pen. The only problem with Mr. Rodriguez was that he liked to talk—a lot.

Leo charged toward the fridge at the side of the store to grab a drink before Mr. Rodriguez could trap him in a conversation. And just in time.

"Olivia, how's Benji?" the storekeeper asked as Leo reached to the back of the cooler to get the coldest soda there was, the plastic bottles slick and cool and delicious on his fingers. "I haven't seen him lately."

"He's only eating a few things right now," Olivia explained. She seemed slightly calmer in the warm, soothing presence of Mr. Rodriguez.

"Perhaps we can find something he'd like," Mr. Rodriguez said. "I will miss him if he stops coming by."

Olivia nodded, but Leo (who was straightening the sodas he'd messed up while grabbing his) could see her glance at the clock display on the counter. And that was when Leo saw that things were much more dire than he'd realized. It was almost noon: The day was slipping away and they were no closer to Nicky! Leo ran to the counter and threw down his root beer, pulling his money out of his pocket so fast the bills fluttered to the floor.

"Slow down there, Leo," Mr. Rodriguez said kindly. "We don't want you losing all your money. And I want to know how your mother's new yoga class is going— she was very excited about it."

It *was* nice how Mr. Rodriguez chatted with anyone he came across and knew everyone in town, but when you were in a hurry, it was seriously bad news. And in this moment it felt like a crisis. Leo glanced at

Olivia, expecting her to rush them out, but just then Gracie stepped forward.

"Mr. Rodriguez, I bet you've been hearing about the terrible thing that happened on our camping trip," she said in her gentle way, placing a hand on the counter. "Nicky was in our cabin and we're really worried about him."

Leo's jaw dropped—what was she doing? Didn't she realize that once he started, Mr. Rodriguez could talk for hours? They were in a rush!

Mr. Rodriguez's face fell. "Such an awful thing," he said. "The poor boy has had such a hard time, and now, when things were finally looking up, this happens." He shook his head, the corners of his mouth turned down.

And now Leo realized what Gracie was doing. She was brilliant! And honestly a little devious. Because if any adult knew what was happening in Snow Valley, it was Mr. Rodriguez. It would seem timid Gracie had another side—a sneaky one.

"What—" Olivia started, but Gracie leaned forward, fully in command of the situation. "I didn't know he had been through a hard time," she said, her voice full of concern. "Though there were incidents last year that made me wonder if he was struggling."

Mr. Rodriguez did something Leo had only ever seen him do with grown-ups, and even then just the ones he liked. He rested his elbows on the counter and ducked his head down. And then he shared what Leo's mom called "the best gossip in town."

"Shari—his mother—struggled when Kip just up and left her with the boy," he began, shaking his head. "She made some awful choices in the past . . . She's doing things right now, working an honest job and taking care of the boy. But it's been rough on him."

Leo had not realized things were so rocky for Nicky—not that it made what he'd done okay, but still.

Gracie nodded wisely and Leo tried to stay still so Mr. Rodriguez wouldn't notice him and remember that he was talking to twelve-year-olds. It was hard because Leo was dying to open his soda. Plus it was kind of hot in the little store, which made his thirst a ball of fire licking at his throat.

"I know he's acted out quite a bit," Mr. Rodriguez said. "But people forgive and kids will be kids."

Leo heard Olivia muffle a snort.

"Anyway, I hope—"

Just then the bell on the door jangled and Mr. Plimpton, who lived down the street from Leo, walked in.

"Julian, hello!" Mr. Rodriguez said, standing up straight and smiling. "How's the leg?"

With that Leo grabbed his soda, making sure one of his dollars made it to the counter to pay for it, and headed out after Olivia, Gracie on his heels.

"Well, that was impressive," Olivia said, turning to Gracie once they hit the sidewalk, the crisp wind refreshing on Leo's cheeks as he opened his soda and chugged, the relief to his throat instant.

"It didn't get us much though," Gracie said, frowning slightly.

"That's really sad about his mom," Leo said.

Even Olivia nodded at this. "Yeah, it sounded pretty bad." Then her face hardened. "But it doesn't make what Nicky did okay."

Leo nodded.

"I wonder—" Gracie began, but Leo suddenly had a nose full of fizz from inhaling the drink, and seconds later he was choking, the soda spraying everywhere.

"Gross, Leo!" Olivia bellowed, then turned and stomped down the sidewalk. The dried leaves crackled under her fierce steps.

Gracie sent him a sympathetic glance, then followed. Neither of them seemed remotely concerned he was hacking up a lung, but once he recovered, he ran to catch up to them on the steps of the Snow Valley Public Library.

Olivia pushed through the big glass doors with such force Leo felt a gust on his face. He gulped the last of his drink, put the bottle in the outside recycling bin, and headed inside.

"That's the enthusiasm I love to see when people enter the library," Ms. MacCullough, the librarian, said. She was sitting behind the circulation desk wearing one of her famous animal print dresses (this one was elephants), her eyes warm as she grinned at them.

Leo grinned back. In books and movies, libraries were quiet, boring places but not in Snow Valley. There was a big computer section with gaming, an incredible craft area, puzzles, Legos, and even a small tumble area for toddlers. It was pretty much the coolest place in town outside the hockey rink. The three of them greeted the librarian, then headed to the back of the huge main room to the rows of tables with computers and heavy wooden chairs.

And there, in the farthest row back, all the way to the right, was Ryan.

CHAPTER 7

GRACIE

Gracie was still feeling shaky as she walked behind Leo and Olivia. The news about Ms. Becker being placed on leave made her stomach ache as though she'd smelled sweaty socks, the one thing still guaranteed to make her puke if she got too close.

If Nicky had been kidnapped and Ms. Becker was fired, it would be Gracie's fault—a thought that was literally making her sick. It also made her even more resolved to see for herself that Nicky was okay. If Olivia was right and he'd run away and they found him, everything would be fine. And if not? Well, Gracie wasn't going to think about that now. Instead she followed as Olivia charged over to Ryan, stepping on someone's backpack as she went.

"Sorry," Gracie said to the man, who was now picking up his bag and glaring at Olivia.

He just shook his head as she slipped past, catching up to Olivia and Leo, who were hovering by Ryan.

". . . talk to us?" Olivia was finishing up her appeal to Ryan.

"Yeah, I'll do whatever I can to help find him," Ryan said, nodding his head but not looking up as he typed. Ryan lived down the block from Gracie. She could remember when he sat on the front steps, refusing to be walked to kindergarten. But somehow between then and now he'd become one of the best hockey players on the school team, a sports reporter for the paper, and head of the middle school Climate Change Club. "So you can ask me anything—but not in here; you never know who's listening."

Gracie glanced around. The only people she saw were the backpack man, who was reabsorbed in his screen, and a few high school guys gaming two rows away. But still, she got Ryan's caution: No one ever knew how Nicky did what he did without getting caught.

"Meet me at one of the benches in front—they're always empty," Ryan said, his fingers still speeding across his keyboard. "I just need to finish this up but I'll be out in a minute."

"Sounds good," Olivia said, immediately striding back down the row. Leo and Gracie followed, Gracie glancing back once at Ryan, noting his fierce concentration as he gazed at the screen.

The long pathway leading up to the library had bright purple benches on both sides, located under trees for protection from the sun in summer. Olivia selected the bench farthest from the library entrance, on the left side, and sure enough no one was nearby. The wind had picked up and Gracie's ponytail smacked her across the face as she sat down.

"Your hair is violent," Leo observed, which made Gracie laugh. Everyone always talked about how beautiful her hair was but, as Leo had said, it definitely had a violent side.

Olivia was staring at the entrance. "What's taking him so long?"

It had been about thirty seconds but Gracie decided not to mention this.

"I was thinking about what Mr. Rodriguez said about Nicky," Leo said, tugging absently at the sleeve of his jacket. "About how he had a hard time but things were getting better because his mom stepped up."

Olivia snorted.

Leo paused, then went on. "I don't think he's actually done anything bad to anyone this year," he said. "Not that I know of."

"Just wait till Ryan gets here," Olivia said. "I'm sure he knows of plenty."

"Maybe," Leo said thoughtfully. "But also a couple of weeks ago I forgot my pencil in math, and you know how Ms. Edwards gets all annoyed when you do that? Nicky was sitting next to me and he gave me an extra pencil. It was nice. Maybe he is changing a little, like Mr. Rodriguez said, because his mom's doing better and stuff."

Gracie had actually been thinking the same thing—not about the pencil, obviously, but that she hadn't heard of Nicky doing anything awful since last spring. *Was* he getting nicer because his mom was better?

"Seriously?" Olivia asked, the word sharp. Clearly she had *not* been thinking the same thing—Gracie was glad she'd stayed quiet. "Nicky goes, what, four weeks without ruining anyone's life that we know of, lends you a pencil, and all of a sudden he's a good guy?"

Gracie inched away from Olivia on the bench.

"Well, no, I was—" Leo sputtered.

"Good, I'm glad to hear you say no because someone as awful as Nicky does not just suddenly get nice," she said, folding her arms across her chest.

"It's just that—" Leo started again.

"Okay," Olivia snarled, standing up to glare at both Leo and Gracie, which did not feel fair—Gracie hadn't said anything! "Let me ask you this: Does a nice guy ask to copy Yasmin's homework, and then when she says no, cyberbully her with memes so bad they were basically legal harassment?"

Gracie had flattened back against the bench in the face of Olivia's rage but she couldn't help gasping at what Olivia had said. Nicky had done some awful things but cyberbullying to the point it was nearly criminal? That was serious.

"Is that what you meant when you said he drove Yasmin's family to move?" Leo asked in a small voice.

Gracie had to admit she'd thought Olivia might be

exaggerating before, but this was truly bad. In health class they'd learned about the impact of cyberbullying on victims and it was scary how much damage it could do.

"Yes," Olivia said shortly, then shook back her bangs and went on. "I mean, her mom wanted to move back to Minneapolis because they have a lot of family there and her dad's company in Albany was downsizing, so the timing was good. But Yasmin's oldest sister was going to be a senior this year and she really wanted to graduate with her class. They went through the Covid shutdown together and everything so they were close. But then Yasmin started getting these emails and no one could trace them, of course, so her parents decided to go—to be surrounded by a kinder community, her mom kept saying—and that was that."

Gracie shook her head. "I can't believe Nicky would do something so cruel," she said.

"Believe it," Ryan said. Gracie jolted back in surprise. She had been so focused on Olivia she hadn't even noticed him approach.

"That's who Nicky is," Ryan said, sitting down next to Gracie, "someone who does cruel things because he feels like it."

"And then gets away with it," Olivia said, sitting back on her edge of the bench. The corners of her mouth were turned down and her eyes were sad.

"Until now, I hope," Ryan said. "If we can find him, that is." Gracie tried to focus but was distracted by the fact that his soap or shampoo had a rich apple scent that stung her nose. She inched back, wishing the breeze would blow the other way. Having an extra-sensitive nose was truly annoying.

Olivia nodded solemnly. "We have to find him if we want that to happen."

"Right, so how can I help you guys track him down?" Ryan asked and ran a hand through his hair, which made the smell worse. Gracie stood up, pretending her leg was falling asleep, so she could move away without being rude and actually listen to Ryan.

"Start with the list," Leo said. "What is it exactly, and what's the plan?"

He spoke in a slightly gruff manner he hadn't used before. Or maybe Gracie just hadn't noticed it.

"People are tired of Nicky never getting caught for the stuff he does," Ryan began. "And a few weeks ago when Nora did that story for the newspaper on a whistle-blower at the photocopy chain in Albany, it got me thinking that's what we needed: a whistleblower, or a group of them, to expose what Nicky's done. He's gotten away with so much, without getting in trouble, but I think that if it's all in one place, the school will have to believe us that he's the one responsible."

Gracie read the school paper every week but had to admit she generally skipped Nora's articles, which were always too long and often on extremely boring topics. So she'd missed the exposé of the photocopy chain. But she was glad Ryan knew about it because a group of whistleblowers was a great idea!

"So I started asking around, seeing who'd had a run-in with Nicky, and then sitting down with them and getting all the details," Ryan said. "I wrote it all in a notebook, just in case Nicky caught wind of it and tried to hack into my computer."

"Smart," Leo said, nodding. He was still using the voice, his arms now folded over his slightly puffed-out chest.

"The plan is for the whole thing to go live on Monday," Ryan went on. "That's what I'm typing up now. But—"

"What do you mean, go live?" Leo interrupted.

"It's going to go up on Socially Safe, the whole document," Ryan said. Socially Safe was the social media site many schools allowed students to use, as it was closely monitored by administrators—at their school it was handled by one of the office aides, Mr. Wilson. "Don't ask me how it can be blasted to everyone at our school at once. I'm not the one handling the tech part."

Gracie was confused. "But what about Mr. Wilson? Won't he take it down as soon as he sees it?"

Ryan grinned. "Well, he has to read it first. And it's being sent at exactly 7:49."

Now all three of them were grinning.

"Brilliant," Olivia said.

It was. At 7:49 a.m., Mr. Wilson was out of the office to open the main doors while most students were doing a final check of their phones before putting them away for the school day. Students were guaranteed to get the notification from Socially Safe and read the document before it could be discovered and taken down.

"But then the other thing is that we *want* Mr. Wilson to see it eventually and show it to Principal Montenegro," Ryan added. "That way Nicky finally gets what's coming to him."

"What's been coming for a long time," Olivia agreed, nodding like a satisfied cat. "Unless Nicky is still missing and everyone's so worried about his safety they don't care what he did in the past."

Now Ryan was frowning as he ran a hand through his hair yet again. Gracie fought the urge to slap it down. "Or he figures out how to stop it."

"Is that possible?" Gracie asked.

Ryan shrugged. "You're asking the wrong person— I'm not the tech guy. But I've definitely learned to never underestimate Nicky—not after all I've heard." He sighed but then looked up at Olivia. "So what's your plan? Because I wouldn't underestimate you either." He grinned at Olivia, who grinned back.

"We want you to tell us everything you know about Nicky," Leo said. He was back using the voice and standing oddly. Gracie now realized what was happening: He was trying to sound cool and nonchalant in front of Ryan.

Ryan cocked his head to the side. "Like what exactly?"

"If we know more about him, maybe we can figure out where he's hiding. And you've talked to all these people, so you probably know him better than anyone else at school," Olivia said. "What are his hobbies, what does he do when he's not ruining lives?"

Gracie leaned forward. "And what are his patterns, and has he deviated from them at all?"

All three of them turned to her, and she could tell they were impressed with the question, which was kind of insulting, actually. Ryan and the others shouldn't underestimate *her*.

"Okay, so first, I was surprised by how many people said Nicky's been paranoid lately," Ryan began. "Like, last week Jamal was asking people where they live because his sister is selling Girl Scout cookies and Nicky said he would never reveal his home address."

Gracie was confused. "But he takes the bus to school—people see where he lives every day."

"Yeah, plus he lives at Cassidy Trailer Park, which even has a map of resident names and their homes so it wouldn't take much of a detective to track him down," Ryan said. "Which was why Jamal thought it was so strange."

"Maybe he didn't want someone at the door selling cookies," Gracie said. She could see Nicky getting rude about something like that.

Ryan shook his head. "Maybe, but I don't think so because he also wouldn't give out his phone number when he and Lisa were doing a project a couple of weeks ago—he said it was confidential. And when I was talking to Juan, he mentioned Nicky's been acting really jumpy lately and yelling at people that they're sneaking up on him."

"Like anyone would do that," Leo muttered.

"Seriously," Ryan agreed. Leo seemed to preen at the praise, smiling wide and standing a little straighter. "And he also screamed at Brian for looking at his computer screen in social studies when they were supposed to be working together." Ryan grinned wryly. "Too bad you can't get your hands on his computer—I'm sure all the answers you need are there."

"Yeah, he took that on the trip," Leo said.

"No surprise there," Ryan said. "Anyway, that's all I can think of—I hope it gives you some ideas."

"Definitely," Olivia said. Gracie glanced at her, not sure what she meant. As far as Gracie could see, Ryan had given them nothing useful at all.

Ryan stood up. "I really hope you find him fast," he said. "For everyone's sake. I mean—even Chloe's impacted by him now and she just moved here two months ago."

Nausea instantly swept through Gracie's belly.

"Yeah, we heard Ms. Becker's on leave," Leo said, glancing at Gracie, who knew she probably looked as ill as she felt.

"Chloe's scared she and her mom might have to move back, and she really hated her old school," Ryan said. "We've been hanging out a lot at the library lately and she came by this morning to tell me because you know how she doesn't have a phone." Ryan frowned. "She was crying and everything."

This was bad. Really, really bad.

"Gracie, are you okay?" Olivia asked, her voice faint

94

through the waves of anxiety that were pounding in Gracie's ears and crashing in her stomach.

"Yeah," she managed to say.

"Okay, then we should get going," Olivia said.

They did need to go and Gracie knew this. And she knew how important—no, *essential*—it was that they find Nicky fast. But for just one second, she closed her eyes.

The truth was that Gracie was not okay, and if Ms. Becker and Chloe had to leave Snow Valley because of what had happened, Gracie would never be okay again.

CHAPTER 8

OLIVIA

Olivia's scalp was prickling and her chest was heating up: two signs she was getting crabby. But who could blame her? Gracie had inexplicably become a zombie, and Leo was the slowest biker in the world. They'd made it sound like they each had a reason to search for Nicky, just like Olivia, but as she pedaled furiously down Grove Street toward Cassidy Trailer Park, where Nicky lived, the two of them were starting to feel like deadweight.

"Where are we even going?" Leo shouted.

And now Leo was being dense—it should have been obvious. "Nicky's house," she shouted back. Because Nicky had tried to hide three things (that they knew of): his home, his computer, and his phone number. And one of these was pretty easy to find and investigate. While she knew Nicky himself likely wouldn't be there, they could scout it out for clues.

"Oh, yeah," Leo said.

The trailer park was just outside town, surrounded by trees and featuring an incredible view of the mountains. Trailers were scattered over the sprawling space, most with lawns and flower beds and lots of kids' toys. Olivia slowed as she reached the main entrance, then stopped her bike in front of the map listing where each resident's trailer was located.

"He's toward the back," she informed Leo when he came up, huffing, a minute later.

"Okay, and—"

Olivia took off before Leo could finish the sentence because what was there to say? Leo could help or not but he wasn't going to slow her down.

Trailer 26 was on the far side of the lot, between a somewhat dilapidated blue trailer on one side and a cheery double-wide with a tiny vegetable garden out front on the other. Olivia parked her bike on the side of the driveway, noting that it was empty, so his mom was likely not home, and stood taking in Nicky's home.

Olivia was not sure what she'd expected from a mom who had been struggling and a son who was a menace to society, but it was not a home this cute. And really, there was no other word but *cute*. The trailer was painted a powdery blue with fluffy white clouds stenciled on the front door. There were three sets of wind chimes, all in the shape of clouds, that rang out as the breeze blew, and a big forsythia bush that still had a few stray yellow flowers. A birdhouse, painted the exact blue of the trailer, hung from a low branch on the oak tree at the edge of the yard, and a mat with a fat yellow duck holding a welcome sign was in front of the door. There were footprints in the lawn and on the steps of the small porch, probably from the police earlier, but the place appeared deserted now.

"You'd think someone nice lived here," Leo said, coming up behind Olivia, who snorted.

"Looks can be deceiving," she said, shaking off her own surprise at all the cuteness and zeroing in on potential hiding spots. Unfortunately there weren't many—the trailer, which was not a double-wide, stood on cement blocks (painted white), so there was no basement. And it was unlikely Nicky planned to hide out in the mucky space between the trailer and the ground, which was about a foot and a half high. There was no attic, obviously, nor was there a shed in the small yard.

"So where could he be?" Leo asked as Gracie walked up, her face weirdly blank.

Why was Leo asking questions instead of making suggestions? Why was Gracie staring off in the distance and not helping? Why did Olivia have to do everything?

"Well, I'm thinking inside the house," she said, her voice oozing sarcasm. She doubted Nicky himself was here (though it could be an evil villain move to hide in the place so obvious no one would look) but for sure there could be clues.

Leo stared at her for a moment. "Right, but maybe there are other places here too, like a common storage unit or something. That's what I was going to say before—that we should look on the map."

Okay, so maybe she was being a little abrupt. And yes, okay, that was a good idea. "Sorry, yeah, that's really smart," she said. "Let's check out the house and then look for common areas." This time she waited until Leo nodded before springing into action, heading to the front door.

She was about to knock when Gracie spoke up, nearly causing Olivia to fall off the small porch from shock. She'd kind of forgotten Gracie could speak.

"Maybe we should just look in the windows," Gracie said softly. Her hair tie had fallen out and her curls were blowing in her face. "On the off chance he's actually there, we want to catch him, not give him time to hide in a closet or whatever."

This was another good idea. Maybe Leo and Gracie weren't deadweight—at least not when they were coming up with stuff like this.

"Good point," Leo said, stepping off the porch as Olivia nodded. "I'll go around and look in the back windows." He took off, trotting around the small trailer.

Gracie headed to look in the windows on the left side of the door, so Olivia headed right. She stood on tiptoe to gaze inside, her eyes taking a moment to adjust to the dim light of the cozy living/dining room area with a little kitchen attached. The first thing she saw was that no one was there. The second thing she saw was what she *didn't* see: There was no obvious evidence of someone having been there in the past few hours. No dishes out, no TV on or gaming remotes out, nothing. Just two denim-covered armchairs, a table with two spindly chairs, a big TV mounted on the far wall, and a bulky gaming system underneath. The small coffee table had a doily and vase with what were probably plastic flowers, given that the vase was empty but the flowers were bright, and several watercolor prints of the ocean decorated the other walls. Olivia was about to step away when suddenly she saw it—a shadow moving across the far side of the room.

Heart racing, Olivia pressed her face to the glass, only to suffer a severe disappointment: The shadow was cast by Leo, staring in the window across from her. When he caught sight of her, he waved. With a sigh Olivia waved back, then walked back into the yard. Gracie was heading toward her.

"Anything?" Olivia asked.

"No sign of anyone in either bedroom," Gracie said, her voice detached. "And they're small rooms—no place to hide."

What was going on with her?

"You guys, I saw something," Leo said, barreling around the house. "Come check it out!"

Olivia raced to catch up with Leo, who led them to a small window at the back of the trailer. "Look."

Olivia stood on tiptoe to peek in. The window

looked into a bedroom but at an angle Gracie would not have seen. Olivia could make out the corner of a bed and a bedside table. The blue blanket was messily pulled across the bed and there was a pile of clothes on the floor. The small bedside table had a lamp and a messy stack of Pokémon cards, along with a half-empty glass of water. It basically just looked like a normal boy's room.

"I don't see anything," she said to Leo as Gracie came up and peered over her shoulder.

"Wait, is that Nicky's computer?" Gracie asked immediately.

Olivia drew in a sharp breath because, yes, it was, right there on the little table! It was kind of embarrassing that she'd missed it, but the real question was, what did it mean?

"I thought you said he had his computer," Olivia said accusingly to Leo as she turned around.

"He did, I swear," Leo said, holding up his hands.

"But this one is definitely his—it has that sticker on it," Gracie said.

She was right: Nicky's computer had a distinctive smiley face sticker—it looked like a regular yellow smiley but the eyes were *x*'s. It was unique and a bit creepy—which could only mean that the computer in the house belonged to Nicky.

"Should we try to get it?" Leo whispered, even though no one else was around.

Olivia was tempted—it could have all the answers they needed—but breaking into a house was illegal.

"I don't—" she began, but before she could finish the sentence, a door slammed behind her, making all of them jump.

"You kids better get out of here!"

Olivia turned and saw an extremely agitated older lady standing on the porch of the trailer next door, one hand on her hip, the other pointing an accusing finger at them. "I can tell you're up to no good and I want you gone quicker than a cat on a mouse or I'm calling the police. That's a good boy living there and he doesn't need hoodlums like you causing trouble."

"We're just leaving, ma'am," Leo called, getting on his bike quite quickly—possibly even quicker than a cat on a mouse. Olivia hastily followed, nearly tripping over her bike.

"I can't believe she thinks *we're* the hoodlums,"

Leo said reproachfully when the three regrouped at the trailer park map.

"And *Nicky's* the good guy," Olivia agreed, shaking her head in disgust.

"I guess we're not getting the computer," Leo said.

"We were *not* going to break into Nicky's house," Gracie said, sounding animated for the first time. "Obviously."

She was right. Olivia wanted—*needed*—to find Nicky but she wasn't going to get arrested along the way.

"So if his computer was at his house, what did he have in his bag?" Olivia asked. This seemed like the best new clue they had found so far.

"Do you think he took a school laptop home and then brought it on the trip?" Leo asked.

"That would make sense," Gracie said.

Olivia nodded. "So his computer is here at his place and he has another one—probably from school—with him. How does this help us?"

No one spoke. Olivia heard a car in the distance, birds chirping, a lawn mower a few trailers away. But nothing from Leo or Gracie. Olivia was silent too because she couldn't make anything of it either. At this point in their investigation, it was like the strange fishing boots: something to file away in case it became significant later.

"Okay," Olivia said with a sigh. "Let's see where else we can search." Just then she heard something close to them, a scraping on the gravel on the side of the road. She glanced toward the bushes that blocked them from the street but didn't see anything.

"It looks like there's a common storage area here," Leo said, pointing to a spot on the map. He hadn't seemed to have noticed the sound—it was probably nothing. "And a shed too, that says 'off-limits,' but we all know Nicky and off-limits." He rolled his eyes.

"Let's go," Olivia said.

The common storage area, a large warehouse, was wide open when they arrived. They headed in and saw long rows of chain-link lockers, each with the name and trailer number of its owner. Leo led them down the two aisles and they peered into each one. Some were empty, some were stuffed with old appliances, toys, and boxes, and none contained Nicky.

The three headed to the off-limits shed next. It was at the front of the park, and as they pulled up close,

Olivia nearly veered off the road into a tree. Because the shed was cordoned off by police tape, a cop car sitting out front.

Leo almost plowed his bike into her. "Did they find Nicky?" he hissed.

Olivia's heart was thumping hard against her ribs, her hands shaking as she parked her bike. Gracie pulled up next to her, her face even more zombie-fied as she tugged off her bike helmet, her eyes glued to the shed. Leo let his bike fall to the ground, then almost tripped over it since he too was staring at the scene before them.

Olivia's breath came in short gasps as she made her way to the cop car and the officer leaning against it.

"Sorry, kids, this is a crime scene so I'm going to have to ask you to leave," the cop said kindly, shading her eyes as she looked at them.

"Is it—did you find Nicky?" Leo choked out.

Olivia now held her breath because this could be it!

"Is that the child who went missing from the school trip?" the officer asked.

Gracie made a small whine of disappointment as Olivia felt her hopes crash at her feet, shattering like a stack of dropped plates.

"Yes," Leo said, his face crestfallen.

"I'm sure you're worried about your friend," the officer said. "And obviously I can't comment on that investigation. But I can tell you that this crime scene does not involve a minor being found."

"Thanks," Olivia managed to say. And the three of them headed back to their bikes.

"Where do we go now?" Leo asked, picking up his bike where it had fallen.

Olivia wanted to tell him to take better care of it but didn't have the heart. She was too discouraged. So she just shrugged and began walking her bike back toward the exit of the trailer park. A red car was turning into the trailer park and Olivia watched to see if maybe it was going to turn into Nicky's drive. Unfortunately it stopped at a trailer a few feet away, but then, just ahead, a biker shot out from a path behind them, racing down the dirt road so fast it created a dust cloud behind him.

"Hey, that's Gus," Leo said, surprised. "What's he doing here?"

Olivia suddenly remembered the sound she had heard earlier. "Is he following us?" she asked.

Leo was glaring after Gus, who was now peeling out of the park. "Probably," he said. "He's always doing dumb stuff to bug people."

Olivia didn't know Gus well but Leo seemed certain. And Leo did hang out with Gus and the other hockey guys a lot, so he'd know—and most of those guys did dumb stuff to bug people, so it fit.

"This has been a huge waste of time," she said, angry at herself for suggesting they come here at all— what supervillain left out obvious clues when they'd gone into hiding? Olivia should have known better.

Gracie did not even appear to be listening and Leo was looking back at the crime scene. Did they not care that half an hour had been lost when the clock was ticking down?

"You know, maybe that crime scene does have something to do with Nicky," Leo said, eyes still on the police officers. "Like, what if he stole something to help with his plan?"

"Oh, that makes sense," Olivia said, impatience evaporating. "What do you think he took?"

Leo shrugged. "It could be anything."

Which was true but not helpful. And with the cops hanging around, it wasn't like they could investigate.

"Where to next?" Leo asked again, looking at her.

Irritation bubbled up in her belly: Why wasn't *he* coming up with a plan?

But then Gracie spoke. "You know how that cop kept calling the shed a crime scene?" she asked, looking the tiniest bit more like herself and less like a zombie.

Olivia nodded. "It made me wonder if we should check out the other crime scene—the one where Nicky disappeared."

"We were at the campground this morning," Leo pointed out.

"And the police already searched it with dogs and everything," Olivia added, rubbing her back, which was starting to itch. This always happened when she biked on a sunny day, no matter how cool it was outside: She sweat, the sweat dried, and then she was itchy. It was very annoying.

"Yeah, it's probably not a good idea," Gracie said. "It's just— We were only at the cabin this morning, and we didn't see the rest of the camp. What if the police missed something?"

That did not seem likely to Olivia. The cops were professionals, after all.

"I think it's worth a shot," Leo agreed.

"I don't think so," Olivia said.

"Do you have a better idea?" Leo asked.

Olivia now wanted to pinch Leo because, no, she did not.

"Yeah, that's what I thought," he said, smug and super annoying. "And we have to do something. Remember, this isn't just about us anymore—we need to find Nicky, or Ms. Becker's and Chloe's lives will be ruined too."

Olivia was about to respond, to take his head off once and for all. But before she could open her mouth, something shocking happened.

Gracie burst into tears.

CHAPTER 9.

LEO

Leo reached out and patted Gracie's shoulder. "It's going to be okay," he said, glancing at Olivia to see if she had any idea why Gracie was now sobbing.

Olivia appeared frozen—she was probably one of those people who freaked out when people cried. Everyone was emotional in Leo's house though, like his sister, who was always in tears over something (usually being told she couldn't wear her tutu to school—or that she had to go to school). So crying did not faze Leo, but he was puzzled why Gracie was this upset. They hadn't failed in uncovering Nicky, not yet anyway.

"It won't be," Gracie snuffled through her tears. "Not if we don't find Nicky."

Leo gave Olivia a quizzical look but Olivia just shook her head. Leo noticed she had her hands in a knot—crying definitely made her uncomfortable.

"I don't understand," he told Gracie. "We're working on it and"—he paused to shoot Olivia a sour look—"I think your idea of checking out the crime scene is a good one."

"Me too," Olivia said so fast Leo had to grin. "Sorry I was crabby about it—I'm just stressed, but really it's a great idea. The best."

Now Leo was trying not to laugh.

But Gracie shook her head and let out a shaky sigh that ended in a hiccup. "No, you just want me to stop crying and I will, it's just—" Her eyes welled again and Olivia took a small step back. "If Ms. Becker loses her job and she and Chloe have to leave, it's going to be all my fault." And now she was bawling again.

"Um, no, it's not," Olivia said, scowling. "It's Nicky's."

"But the whole Nicky thing—him disappearing—*that's* my fault."

Was *Gracie* the mastermind behind all this, the one who plotted and then in the dead of night had Nicky silently kidnapped from their bunk? Leo could tell Olivia was thinking the same thing by how wide her eyes had gotten.

"Are you behind Nicky's disappearance?" he asked breathlessly. This was a plot twist he hadn't seen coming!

Gracie snorted. "Of course not," she said, wiping tears from her cheeks. "I'm not a kidnapper."

Was it wrong that Leo was slightly disappointed by this?

"But if Nicky was kidnapped, if that's what actually did happen, then the kidnapper got in because of me," Gracie said, running a hand under her nose. "I broke the rule about not leaving the cabin after lights out." Her eyes were welling yet again and her voice wobbled. "I had to use the bathroom and didn't want to bother Ms. Becker because she was totally fast asleep, so I just snuck out and I forgot to lock the door when I got back. I heard the police talking about it after my interview this morning, saying that it was weird how the door was unlocked and that's how a kidnapper could have gotten in without making noise. So if—if Nicky was kidnapped by some family member who isn't supposed to have him, the kidnapper got in our cabin because of me, which would mean Ms. Becker getting fired is all my fault."

A car drove past, slowing down and giving the three of them a wide berth. Leo watched but barely saw because he was considering what Gracie had said. Leaving the door unlocked like that in the middle of the night—it wasn't great. The teachers had been really clear about that. No wonder she was so eager to find out what had really happened: If Nicky had planned the whole thing, Gracie was off the hook. But if he had been kidnapped, then sooner or later the police would want to know who had left that door unlocked, making it easy for someone to slip inside late in the night. And the person who had done that was Gracie.

"He wasn't kidnapped," Olivia said, walking over to Gracie and looking her right in the eye. They were the same height (both taller than Leo), which he hadn't fully put together until right now—somehow Olivia had always seemed taller than Gracie. "He's trying to find a way to get out of consequences for that list. He couldn't hack his way in so he's working on something else. I promise. And I never, ever make a promise unless it's for real." There was an intensity in her voice that Leo found inspiring. And Gracie must have felt the same.

"Okay," she said, rubbing her eyes and trying to smile. "Okay."

"And now we go find him," Leo declared, wanting to be part of the moment. He turned and immediately walked into Olivia's bike, which kind of hurt, though not as much as his pride did when both girls laughed.

"Why do you stand it up like that?" he huffed, going over to grab his bike, which was where a normal person would leave it—on the ground. His helmet had rolled a few feet away so he picked that up first. His shin hurt where he'd slammed it on the bike pedal, but he didn't want to rub it. Not that Olivia or Gracie would hassle him about it like the guys would, but Leo was the kind of guy who shook off pain. Or at least he wanted to be, though it was harder than it looked, so he compromised by rubbing it gently with his other leg.

"It's called taking care of your stuff," Olivia said, heavy on the sarcasm, as she scratched her back. "You should try it."

Like Leo was interested in Olivia telling him what to do. He pulled up his bike, got on, and pedaled off, the girls right behind him. They coasted out of the trailer park, then turned right on Winding Valley Road. Minutes later they had turned onto Kappa Path for the bumpy ride to Frost Peak Campground.

Gracie was first out of the forest twenty minutes later. It turned out that she had another secret superpower besides her sense of smell: not getting tired biking up hills. Both Olivia and Leo were puffing a bit (okay, he was puffing a lot) when they reached the bike rack in front of the main lodge.

"Mountain Lion's our first stop?" Leo asked, cheerful again despite the fact he was kind of sweaty. The peaceful ride through the woods had calmed him down and he was feeling more optimistic. He stuffed his bike into the rack, where it half stood, half sagged sideways.

Olivia nodded and made a big point of settling her bike on the kickstand.

"I was thinking more about the clues we've found so far," Gracie began, hooking her helmet over her handlebars. Her bike was also supported by the kickstand but she didn't make a big thing of it. "I think Nicky using a school computer fits with what Ryan said about him being paranoid—Nicky doesn't want anything he's doing, or anything he's done, being tracked by someone online."

"Makes sense," Leo said, because it did though he didn't see how that helped them. But it seemed like confessing her secret had unburdened Gracie and made her a little more talkative and that was definitely good.

"So if he thinks he's being tracked or spied on, like Ryan said, and he's worried about being caught, maybe he ran away so he could thwart Ryan's plan. No one would be able to see him—online or in person—and stop him."

Leo nodded excitedly. Everything she was saying made sense, and the clues were fitting together.

"Yeah, that tracks," Olivia said. "But it doesn't tell us where he went."

Gracie blinked a few times and nodded, her shoulders slumping a bit. Leo felt bad for her—Olivia could really be a bummer.

"It's still great though," Olivia added, probably realizing she'd been harsh. And also probably not wanting to make Gracie cry again.

Gracie shrugged. "Maybe it'll be helpful later," she said. "When we find out more."

"And speaking of, let's get going to Mountain Lion," Olivia said.

The sun was bright and Leo was still warm from their ride, so he pulled off his jacket and tossed it onto the ground beside his bike before following the girls.

"No littering!" someone shouted. Leo jumped a mile. He turned and saw a man with a scraggly beard in a Snow Valley Campground shirt walking toward him. The guy had small eyes and a beak-like nose and was swinging his arms like he was about to start racing. "Pick that up!"

Leo was unsure what was going on. "Ah, this is just my coat and I was—"

"Pick it up!" the guy said. He spoke very precisely and for a second Leo wondered if this was an elaborate prank.

"Okay," Leo said, snatching up his jacket. "Is this a joke?"

"Littering is never a joke," the man said, then shuffled off into the lodge.

"What a weirdo," Leo said, baffled by what had just taken place.

"Don't call him that!" Olivia shouted.

Leo jumped and Gracie let out a small cry of surprise.

"Um, sorry," Leo said, not sure why he had been yelled at—calling a jacket litter *was* weird.

Olivia pressed her lips and shook her head like Leo was hopeless. He still didn't understand and he was getting sick of how Olivia kept snapping all the time. He was about to hurry them along to Mountain Lion when there was a sharp rustling in the bushes behind him. "Did you guys hear that?" he asked, his pulse quickening. The campground was deserted, besides the angry employee. What if a family of bears had come to see if there were any food scraps around?

Olivia rolled her eyes so hard it must have hurt. "It was just a squirrel," she said. "Or something."

Leo wanted to point out that the "something" could be a bear but that would make him look wimpy so he chose another angle. "What if someone is following us?" And then it hit him. "What if *Nicky* is following us? What if he found out we're tracking him and is planning to lure us into the woods?"

"And do what?" Olivia asked, her voice so full of scorn Gracie winced and gave Leo a sympathetic look.

"I don't know," Leo said irritably. "Something bad."

Olivia glared. "You are not taking this seriously," she said, each word pointed.

"I am," he said, stung.

"You're not acting like it," Olivia said, eyes flashing. "You don't have any ideas, you come up with stupid theories—I don't think you really care if we find Nicky—not like me and Gracie, who actually have an investment in stopping Nicky before he gets away scot-free again."

"I'm invested," Leo said, and now he was angry too. "You have no idea how badly I need to find Nicky."

"So tell me," Olivia demanded, hands on hips. "Why do you care so much about exposing Nicky?"

Leo had had it with Olivia and her scorn. "He stole a knife from me," he nearly shouted. "And I need it back or my brother will kill me."

Sure enough, Olivia's mocking look slipped right off her face.

Was she satisfied now that she knew how serious Leo's situation actually was? Not that she could ever fully get it. Leo and Noah were close, they rarely argued, they had fun hanging out, and they never, ever took each other's stuff without asking. But the knife—it wasn't just that it was Noah's, it was that it was his prize possession. Noah was a hard-core climber and one of the tools of the sport was a small folding knife: sleek, compact, and razor-sharp. Noah had begged to be allowed to carry one, and once he got permission to get one after his fifteenth birthday, he had saved every penny from his allowance and the lawns he mowed until he had enough. It was only last month that he'd finally purchased the Mountaineer Rope Saw. He hadn't even used it yet! But when Steve and the guys were discussing climbing, Leo had seen an opportunity to impress them, show he was part of the group. Did Leo lie and say the knife was his? Did he then get pressured to show it to them? Did he then agree to bring it on the trip? Yes, yes, and yes. And did he regret that choice a million times but never more than the moment when he opened his backpack and saw it was missing? Again, yes.

Nicky had gone through Leo's backpack, discovered the knife, and taken it. That's why Leo's backpack had been moved from where he'd left it. And if Leo went home without the knife and Noah discovered it was gone, well, it was just too awful to consider what might happen next. His brother would never forgive him. Which was why Leo *had* to find Nicky and get Noah's knife back.

"Um, okay, I didn't expect that," Olivia said, blinking a few times.

"Because you just assume stuff about people," Leo said, sulking a little. In fairness, most people had assumptions about Leo but Olivia was particularly quick to judge.

"He's not wrong," Gracie said, twisting her ponytail.

It was difficult to say who was most shocked by this: Leo, Olivia, or Gracie herself. Since when did she start speaking up? Leo wasn't sure but he was a fan.

Gracie turned to Leo. "I bet your brother will understand," she said.

The worst part was that he probably would. Noah got Leo and all the dumb stuff he did. But that was the problem—Leo was always doing dumb stuff and Noah deserved better.

Olivia was looking at him shrewdly. "You can also try to make it up to him," she said. "Not just say you're sorry but show him."

That was interesting. "How?"

Olivia shrugged. "Maybe go on a hike with him and pack a picnic."

That would probably be more fun for Leo than Noah but Leo appreciated that Olivia was thinking about it. "We've done a lot of hiking together," he said, wanting to give a positive response. "When I was a kid, we had this game where he'd go first and I'd try to only step in his footprints."

"That's sweet," Gracie said, smiling genuinely. But then her expression changed abruptly, her eyes widening and her mouth tight. "But wait—does this mean Nicky is armed with a knife?"

Leo nodded. "Yeah," he said slowly. "I don't think he'd use it—he's never been violent before, but—"

"But we can't assume he won't use it if threatened," Olivia finished.

"Right," Leo said. Gracie was biting her lip, clearly imagining worst-case scenarios, but Leo really didn't believe Nicky would hurt them with a weapon—it just wasn't how he operated, or needed to. Though obviously if they found Nicky and he brandished the knife, Leo would be out of there fast.

"So we proceed with extra caution," Olivia said. She was tugging at her jacket sleeve, clearly ready to move on.

"Let's get going," Leo said, because after all, the clock was ticking.

The path twined past Eagle and Owl cabins, the soft swirling of Coldwater Creek and chirping birds the only sounds nearby. The sun sparkled over the mountain peaks in the distance, which got Leo thinking even more about those hikes with Noah, the fun of stepping in his prints as they trod up the mountainside.

"We're here," Olivia announced unnecessarily when they'd passed the bathrooms and turned the corner to Mountain Lion. Leo wasn't sure what he'd expected, probably something more like the shed back at Cassidy Trailer Park: yellow tape and maybe the lingering scent of investigation. But the cabin looked the same as it had this morning when they left, no sign of tape or scent of investigation. "I know the police searched all the cabins but let's go inside just in case."

Leo headed up the porch and to the room where he'd slept with Nicky. As expected, it had been swept clean. The bunk bed, small table, and lamp were the only furniture, and nothing else—not even a stray leaf or bit of dirt—remained. There were a few scuffs on the floor, one a muted red that might have been made by Nicky's rubber boots. Leo had the same ones and they were always leaving scuffs if he wasn't careful.

"Okay, so what's next?" Olivia asked as they stepped back out onto the porch.

Leo didn't answer because something was starting to come together in his brain. Something about footprints and boots. And Nicky.

"Maybe Nicky dropped something in the woods that the police didn't find?" Gracie asked, not sounding optimistic. "Something that could help us track him?"

And then it clicked. "Rubber boots leave a distinctive footprint."

Olivia and Gracie turned.

"What?" Olivia asked, her brows crinkling.

It was so simple. "Rubber boots leave a distinctive print, which means Nicky's boots left prints," Leo said, spreading out his hands. "Prints we can follow to track him." Just like Leo had followed his brother's prints.

For the first time Olivia beamed, her smile radiant. "That is brilliant!" she said.

Gracie nodded and patted Leo's arm. "It really is."

Leo wasn't sure two compliments had ever meant more. "Thanks," he said, his insides glowy and warm.

"And you know what?" Gracie asked, sounding even more excited. "The police wouldn't have known to look for those prints because they don't know about the boots."

"Excellent point," Olivia said gleefully, rubbing her hands together. "We're the only ones with this intel!"

For the first time ever Leo knew what it felt like to be a superhero.

"Okay," Olivia said as she turned, surveilling the cabin. "Let's get to it. He'd have either come out the window on his side or the door. So let's start looking there."

Leo headed to the window while the girls stayed near the front porch. He bent down, looking for prints. On the plus side it had rained a lot this past week, so the ground was spongy enough to hold prints made recently. But on the not-plus side, Leo didn't find any. He walked a few feet away, knelt down, and tried again. Nothing. Maybe this wasn't such a great idea.

"I think I found something," Gracie called.

Leo hurried over to where she stood and sure enough there it was. The unique print of the boot—even horizontal lines with a circle in the middle—was embedded a few feet from the porch.

"Let's follow them," Olivia said.

It was harder at the front of the cabin, where the police, as well as Leo, Olivia, Gracie, and Ms. Becker, had also walked, but they were able to follow the trail around the back of the cabin and then it became easier.

"This is so great," Olivia told Gracie as they crouched low, moving from print to print. "We're totally going to find him."

Leo had to admit he was feeling pretty excited himself as the prints wove deeper into the woods, where the sounds of birds, the creek, and scuffling animals surrounded them. Leo tried not to think about what some of those animals might be.

And then up ahead he heard Olivia call out.

He straightened and made his way through bushes and underbrush to where she stood with Gracie at the edge of the creek, both dejected. They didn't have to explain why: Leo could see that the prints led straight into the water. Nicky had worn rubber boots for this exact purpose—to wade through the creek to his final hideaway. Because police dogs couldn't track his smell once he entered the water.

It was yet another dead end.

CHAPTER 10

GRACIE

"Okay," Gracie said, taking a deep breath. "I know this is a hit but we need to keep searching."

Leo nodded with none of his usual energy.

Olivia gave a half shrug.

This would not do. They *had* to keep going. "Here's the plan," she announced. "We're going to follow the creek and look for any sign of someone coming out of the water. Because at some point Nicky had to get out."

"The bushes and stuff are too dense," Olivia pointed out.

That was true—they weren't going to be able to walk right along the creek. But the path followed it pretty closely and they could duck into the woods and check in places with a little more space between trees.

So that was what they did, Gracie leading the way. No one spoke and the silence was heavy. Not that it was ever really silent in the woods of course—there were birds, the muffled sounds of chipmunks and squir-rels, and the whisper of leaves as the breeze blew. The air smelled like fall: crunchy leaves, smoke from the fire-place at the lodge, and the tiniest hint of snow holding the promise of winter. But then Gracie caught a whiff of a new scent, one that got stronger as they rounded the bend and neared Cobra cabin.

"Something smells off in that cabin," Gracie said, her nose scrunching. *Off* wasn't actually the word for the aroma wafting toward her from Cobra: *vile* and *disgusting* were more accurate. It smelled, inexplicably, like her nose nemesis: filthy, sweaty socks.

Olivia sniffed loudly, then glanced quizzically at Gracie. "I don't smell anything. Let's just keep going."

"It might be dangerous in there," Leo added. "Remember Ms. Becker said it was off-limits."

But Gracie smelled something and she needed to know what it was. "I'll just be a second," she told them.

She strode up the small path to Cobra, ducking under the rope and past the DO NOT ENTER: CONSTRUC-TION ZONE sign hanging on the porch rail. Her feet were strong and sure as she marched up the steps, twisted the doorknob, and stepped inside.

And then let out an ear-piercing scream.

Olivia was behind her immediately, close and comforting and smelling of lilac body wash. "What is it?" she asked, her voice steel.

Despite her terrible shock, Gracie could not help but appreciate that Olivia had rushed toward Gracie's scream, not away. Whatever had happened, Olivia was not deserting her to handle it alone.

And Gracie did not need to explain because Olivia was suddenly gripping Gracie's upper arm so hard she winced: Olivia had just seen what was in the cabin.

Or more accurately, *who* was in the cabin.

"Nicky!" Olivia roared. "Are you kidding me?"

Because the cause of Gracie's scream was indeed Nicky. He had been lying on the front-room bed doing something on his phone, which had fallen to the floor when he'd leapt up at Gracie's scream.

"Careful, he has a weapon!" Leo shouted as he sprinted in, waving his arms.

"What are you doing here?" Nicky asked, his eyes darting back and forth. Gracie noted his brown hair was matted to one side and his pale, freckled face was tinged pink, probably from surprise. "And I don't have a weapon," he added, looking at Leo as though he'd gone bananas. Then he looked back at Olivia. "Are the police with you?"

"What are *you* doing here?" Olivia hissed through clenched teeth, hands on her hips. "And no, they aren't, not yet."

"How did you find me?" Nicky demanded. He was wearing jeans and a sweatshirt that were wrinkled, as if he had spent the night sleeping in them. The cabin looked like Mountain Lion, with the single bed in this front room, where Nicky had clearly set up camp. His backpack was in the corner, with a shirt and socks—the socks Gracie had smelled—crumpled on the floor next to it. Several wrappers and empty water bottles were scattered around.

"How did the police *not* find you?" Gracie asked, stepping forward, but no closer to the socks—she couldn't risk puking.

Nicky rubbed his eyes for a moment. "I wasn't here until the police left. Before that I was downstream, waiting for them to clear out." He gestured to the pair of beat-up rubber fishing boots in the corner, still damp on the toes.

"You were downstream, right," Olivia said, voice thick with anger, "hiding from the dogs you knew would come when you concocted this evil plan."

"Well, yeah, dogs can't sniff you out in water," Nicky said matter-of-factly as he sat back down on the bed. "And there was no way I was going to risk them finding me." He looked up at them. "So why are you here?"

"We're looking for you, duh," Leo snapped. He was clearly trying to regain dignity after the weapon thing.

"Why?" Nicky asked, seeming genuinely puzzled. He had dark circles under his eyes and his nails were bitten down to the quick.

Gracie was surprised by this response.

"Because it's time for you to pay for the things you've done," Olivia said archly, Leo nodding in satisfaction.

"We know about the list Ryan put together," Gracie told him.

To her great surprise, he laughed. "Oh, yeah, right, the big exposé. No, I'm not worried about that."

"Right, like—" Olivia began, voice hostile, but

Gracie held up a hand and gave her a look. Nicky's statement had her curious and she wanted to know what he meant.

"You're not worried about all the mean stuff you did being revealed on Socially Safe," she half asked, half stated.

Nicky sighed. "It's not like I'm happy about it but it had to happen sometime, right? And listen, I know you won't believe me but I'm sorry about a lot of what I did. Things weren't good for me back then but it's different now, better, and I've already been thinking about apologizing for a lot of it."

Olivia let out a burst of icy laughter. "Like I believe that," she hissed.

Gracie shot her another look. Nicky sounded genuine to her and, sure, he could have been lying but what if he wasn't? What if there was something more going on? If there was, Gracie wanted to know about it.

Olivia shook her head but then raised her hands and stopped speaking, allowing Gracie to take charge.

"So then why are you hiding?" Gracie asked Nicky.

"I'm being framed for something," Nicky said.

"Right," Olivia scoffed, laughing a loud, very

unamused laugh as she narrowed her eyes in a way that could only be described as threatening, while Leo snorted in disbelief.

Gracie gave them both a sharp look. Then she stepped closer to Nicky. "What?" she asked.

Nicky bit his lip for a moment. "I'm being framed for trying to breach the school firewall."

Gracie looked at him blankly because this was not what she had expected, and wasn't it almost impossible to breach a firewall? "Explain," she told him.

Nicky ran a hand through his messy hair, ruffling it even more. "I was doing my weekly email security check—" he began.

"What's that?" Leo interrupted.

"If you're worried about being hacked, which you guys probably aren't, it makes sense to check your settings and history and stuff," Nicky said. "Especially because lately I've been seeing little things that made me wonder if someone had gotten into my files. And then yesterday I found traces of an email I hadn't sent but that had gone out from my account."

Gracie hadn't known that could happen.

"It's a very tough hack if someone changes their

password regularly, which I do," he added, now picking a cuticle. "So this person has skills."

"You would know," Olivia muttered.

Nicky snickered, then continued, "This kind of email they sent, it's called spear phishing. It's a well-researched, targeted message, and when someone opens it, it injects malware into the admin system. It went out Friday night so it's there now, just waiting for Principal Montenegro or someone else in the office to open it first thing Monday, get hacked, and trace it back to me."

Gracie was losing the thread but it didn't matter—she got enough to understand Nicky's fears. And now she had questions.

"So you think someone's following you, not just online but in real life too?" Gracie answered, checking if her guess from earlier this afternoon was correct. "And that's why you ran away."

Olivia snorted at this.

"Yeah, but it's not just something I'm imagining, someone's really tracking me," he said, glaring at Olivia. "That's part of how they got into my account—they put some kind of malware in my computer or spied at school to get my password—I don't know. But they've been at it for weeks and, yeah, not just online."

"What do you mean?" Leo asked, the corners of his mouth turning down. Gracie could tell just hearing about this was spooking him—for all he tried to act tough, Leo was pretty sensitive.

Nicky sighed and bit his lip for a moment. "A few weeks ago, right before this all started, someone was trying to get in the window. I think they thought no one was home because Mom was out and I was gaming and hadn't turned on the light. But I heard them and saw someone running across the yard when I got there." The anxiety in his voice seemed real, and he paused to pick at a nail that was already chewed down to the skin. "And then a few days later my neighbor said someone was lurking around the house when Mom and I were out. So yeah, I wasn't going to be at home like a sitting duck for this person to just come and find me."

"And do what?" Leo asked, eyes wide.

Nicky smiled wryly. "I wasn't going to wait and find out, not when I need to focus on hacking this hack."

"So your plan is to hide out in Cobra forever? I don't think that's going to work out," Gracie said.

"Duh," Nicky snapped.

"Don't talk to Gracie like that," Olivia warned him, lips pursed.

Gracie was surprised by this—and warmed that Olivia would defend her.

"Sorry," Nicky said.

Gracie's jaw dropped. Nicky apologizing? This had never happened.

"I just—no, my plan isn't relocating to Cobra for the rest of my life. My plan is to undo this hack and then figure out who's behind it." He gestured to a lump on the bed that Gracie hadn't noticed before but now saw was a school computer.

"How's it going?" she asked, curious.

Nicky shook his head, his eyes clouding. "Not well," he said. "This hacker is out of my league. But I have to keep trying."

"Actually . . ." Olivia started stepping forward, but Leo cut her off.

"Where's my knife?"

Nicky appeared puzzled by this and then annoyed. "I have no idea what you're talking about."

"My knife," Leo said insistently. "The one you took out of my backpack in the cabin last night."

Nicky shook his head. "I didn't touch your bag or your knife. Why would I need a weapon to uncover a hack?"

"To protect yourself from snakes or mountain lions out here in the woods," Leo said, like it was obvious.

Nicky laughed rudely. "You have to be kidding—I have better things to do than make up dumb stuff to worry about."

Leo glowered at him and Gracie could tell Nicky's remark had shamed him. "Okay, so then to protect yourself from this stalker who was lurking around your house, in case they find you here. I think you're lying about my knife," he persisted.

"And I think your time is up," Olivia said coolly, arms folded over her chest. She had clearly come to the end of her rope and, honestly, Gracie wasn't sure what else there was to say. Olivia had guessed correctly: Nicky was hiding out to slither his way out of getting in trouble again. But—

But didn't it matter that this time it wasn't trouble

he'd made for someone else? That this time he was being set up to get caught for something he didn't do?

"We'll be heading out now to call the police." Olivia plucked up the rubber boots. "And no wading away so easily this time."

Gracie wondered if she should try to stop Olivia but maybe she was right—maybe it was time to call the police.

"You can't!" Nicky cried as he jumped back up, fists clenched.

"Oh, but I can, and I will," Olivia said vengefully as she wrenched open the cabin door.

Gracie glanced at Leo, who shrugged, nodded, and followed Olivia, then at Nicky, whose face had crumpled.

"I—" she began.

But Olivia had turned and was glaring daggers at Nicky, boots between her fingers. "You're going down, Nicky, and it's what you deserve."

CHAPTER 11

OLIVIA

Olivia's insides were on fire, the furnace that had been lit when Yasmin left flaring up hot and bright. How dare Nicky act like some kind of victim when half the things he'd done were exactly what was happening to him now: Framing someone? Were they supposed to feel sorry for him, excuse the pain he'd inflicted, his cruelty? Just the thought made the flames rise even higher inside her.

"Wait a second."

It was Gracie.

"For what?" Olivia spat out, stomping on a stick in the path, which cracked with a satisfying crunch. "I'll wait when the police are on their way." Though of course they couldn't get too far from the cabin, just in case Nicky tried to flee in his socks.

"No, really, hold up," Gracie said with surprising force.

Olivia spun around. "What?" she shouted.

Gracie, who was right behind her, stopped short to avoid running into Olivia, and Leo, who was next to her, scooted off to the side with surprising speed.

"No yelling!"

All three of them jumped, then turned to see who had spoken. It was the man from before, the one Leo had called a weirdo. He walked with a slight hitch that did not seem to slow him down at all because he was nearing them quite quickly.

"Who are you?" Olivia asked, trying to sound braver than she felt because the man was glaring laser beams of fury at them.

"I am Otto and I take care of things here," he snapped at her. There was something oddly formal about how he spoke, even when he was taking their heads off. "*Care* means everything is safe for the plants and animals, and you yelling—that is not safe. So stop now."

Otto *was* wearing a Snow Valley Campground shirt and green work pants so clearly he was telling the truth.

"Got it, we'll keep our voices down," Leo said in a

soothing voice. Olivia had started to get the impression that Leo was used to people losing it because he had been very calm when Gracie had her meltdown and had never seemed that fazed by Olivia's anger.

"We promise," Gracie added sweetly.

Otto looked from her to Leo and his stance relaxed the tiniest bit. "And you will make sure she is quiet," he said, jerking an elbow toward Olivia, who could not help being offended.

"I can keep my voice down," she informed him frostily.

"Then show me," Otto snapped, glaring at her for one final minute and then heading back down the path toward the lodge.

"Okay, you have to admit that guy is weird," Leo said softly, looking after Otto.

"He kind of is," Gracie agreed. "I mean—"

"Don't call him weird," Olivia said, her voice low but her whole body radiating fury.

"Can you say more?" Leo asked, calm and mature and clearly repeating something he had heard or been told many times by a parent. A patient parent. "Because I don't get why you're so mad."

For a moment all Olivia wanted was to scream at Leo and then run like the wind to report Nicky to the police. But both Leo and Gracie were looking at her like it mattered that she was angry—like they did actually want her to say more. And so, to her surprise, she did.

"That's what people call my brother, Benji," she said. "And I hate it."

"That's so mean," Gracie said, and she sounded angry. "No five-year-old is weird."

At the compassion in her voice something drained from Olivia, something that had kept her upright and moving fast: her anger. And without it she found it hard to stand. So she didn't. She plonked down right on the path, dropped Nicky's footwear, and rested her head in her hands.

"Benji kind of is weird though," she nearly whispered. "He does things that aren't normal, and isn't that what weird is?"

Both Gracie and Leo sat right down next to her but stayed silent. Olivia looked up and realized they were considering her question—they wanted to give her a real answer. Which made a new feeling, warm but not hot, cozy but not stifling, start swirling in Olivia's belly.

"I think it's like the difference between calling someone smart versus calling them a know-it-all," Gracie said finally, absently twirling a curl around her fingers. "They're basically the same thing but one has an implied insult and the other doesn't. So, like, if people call your brother nonconforming or whatever, it's just how he acts. But weird means he's bad."

"Neurodiverse," Olivia said as she thought about what Gracie had said.

"What?" Gracie asked, brows scrunching.

"*Neurodiverse* is what you say when someone's brain isn't like other brains," Olivia explained, still mulling over what Gracie had said.

But now Leo was frowning. "Aren't all brains different? Like my brother's all into math and that's how he thinks but my parents say it's fine I think differently."

"How do you think?" Gracie asked.

Leo grinned. "In comics of course."

Olivia grabbed the stick she had stepped on and poked one end of it into the dirt. "You're right, Benji's not weird, he just understands the world differently.

But . . ." She paused, unsure she was ready to say what she had long felt but never spoken, then forged on. "I'm scared people are going to judge him for things he can't control. Because the stuff he does—sometimes it freaks people out, because if he's running and yelling, you're not sure what he's going to do next."

"Why does he run and yell?" Leo asked, swatting at a bee that was several feet away and posed no threat to them.

"Because he's hungry or tired or a kid at the playground took a toy he was playing with—that's the problem—we don't always know so it's hard to fix it until he chills and tells you," Olivia said, poking at the ground a bit more aggressively. "Which is not awful now when he's little and his preschool knows how to help him and the other kids can't bother him too much. But what about next year in kindergarten? And the year after that? You guys know kids just get meaner as they get older."

"Fact," Leo agreed, and Gracie nodded.

"I'm scared," Olivia admitted, and to her horror her voice broke. "I just—I don't want people to be cruel to my brother."

Gracie reached out and held her hand while Leo leaned over to pat her back. Neither of them said anything, which she was grateful for. She couldn't have handled any fake reassurance. Because the truth was that people sometimes would be cruel, and the worst part? There was nothing Olivia could do to stop it.

"I used to bite people," Gracie said suddenly.

"You what?!" Leo asked, sounding as taken aback as Olivia was feeling.

"In preschool," Gracie said. "I bit people—a lot. They almost threw me out of the school actually." She was grinning at the expression on Leo's face—he was clearly aghast, as was Olivia.

"That is very hard to imagine," Olivia informed Gracie.

Gracie smirked. "I know," she said. Then she looked seriously at Olivia. "But I had reasons for doing it, just like Benji has reasons for behaving the way he does. And . . ." She stopped for a moment, but then went on. ". . . like Nicky did."

Olivia leapt to her feet, anger flooding her so fast she was at risk of short-circuiting. "Are you seriously comparing my brother to that—that monster?" she hissed.

Gracie stood up and nodded. "I am because, Olivia, lots of people are like Benji. Maybe it's because their brains work differently like his, or maybe it's because someone was hurting them so they lashed out. That's why I bit kids—there was a boy who was stealing my snacks and pinching me to make me not tell. Everyone has reasons for doing what they do, you know?"

"Even the snack-stealing pincher?" Leo asked, clearly trying to diffuse the tension with a joke.

It didn't work, at least not on Olivia. "My brother is nothing like Nicky," she said coldly.

"But what if Nicky is like me? He felt so bad he had to lash out," Gracie said. "Like I did when I bit other kids."

Olivia could not believe how much she herself wanted to bite Gracie right now. Mostly because it was possible Gracie was right. Then Olivia realized something odd: She wasn't angry anymore. The anger had blown through her and was gone. Which was not like her—she generally stayed mad for the duration of an argument, and at times even longer. But something had happened when she'd shared her fears about Benji with Gracie and Leo. Olivia wasn't quite sure what that was or why it had happened; she only knew that it was a little easier to breathe now than it had been before and that her body felt cool instead of on fire. It felt good.

Not that it made her any less irritated that her friends were defending Nicky.

"So you think Nicky had reasons for doing awful things to other students for two years?" Olivia asked, raising a brow.

Gracie shrugged. "It's probably worth finding out, especially if he really has been planning to apologize," she said. "Remember how Mr. Rodriguez said Nicky had had a hard time?"

"That neighbor said it too," Leo added. "At the trailer park."

Olivia gave him a sour look for being on Gracie's side and he raised his hands in a "what can I do?" gesture.

Olivia shook her head, then glanced past both of them to the cabin where her nemesis, the boy who had driven away her best friend, was plotting to get out of trouble yet again. But—but Gracie was right. It irked Olivia to admit it but everyone did have a story, a reason for what they did. And sometimes— just sometimes—that reason made you see everything differently. Would that happen with Nicky? Olivia doubted it. She *highly* doubted it. But could they spare ten minutes to be sure—absolutely sure—there wasn't some central piece to this story they were missing, some piece that would change everything? Yes. Yes, they could. *She* could.

"Fine," Olivia huffed, scooping up Nicky's shoes and stalking back toward stupid Cobra where stupid Nicky was hiding out. "But if there isn't a really, really, REALLY good reason, we are going to the police!"

CHAPTER 12

LEO

Leo wasn't thrilled that they were headed back up the steps of Cobra, but the girls hadn't exactly consulted him. It probably was the right thing to do but that didn't mean he was looking forward to dealing with Nicky again.

"That was fast," Nicky said, not looking up from the bed where he sat with his laptop perched on his lap, scrolling furiously. "So the police are on their way and you came to rub it in my face?"

"No," Gracie said, coming to a stop in the center of the room and appearing perfectly calm. Leo realized she was no longer as fearful as she'd seemed that morning and he admired how unintimidated she was by Nicky. It was a feeling he did not share.

"Well, not yet," Olivia interjected forcefully. Her cheeks were pink but Leo noticed her voice wasn't quite as harsh as before, and for once she wasn't clenching her fists.

Nicky looked up. "So why are you here?" His glance strayed to Leo. "If you're still looking for your stupid knife, I don't know how many times I have to tell you, I don't have it."

Leo scowled. "It's not stupid—it's my brother's prize possession." Ugh, he wished he hadn't said that, but when he was nervous he babbled. It was another habit Steve and the guys made fun of.

Nicky shrugged, attention back to his computer. "Then I guess he's the stupid one for letting you take it on this trip."

"He didn't let me, I just took it," Leo snapped. Again, why was he sharing this?

"Oh, I get it," Nicky said in a smug voice, looking up at Leo in a way that made Leo want to pinch him. "You're trying to show your friend Steve how tough you are." He raised his top lip in a sneer. "Good luck with that."

"You really are a jerk," Leo snapped. How had Nicky guessed that this was exactly why Leo had taken the knife? Well, actually Nicky had most likely figured it out because Leo had blathered so much about it.

"Me? The jerk is that guy you think is your friend," Nicky snapped back.

"Right, you just think that because he hates you—like everyone else at school," Leo taunted.

"Hey—" Gracie interjected, probably trying to save Leo from himself.

"No," Nicky interrupted, his voice ice. "Because he said my mom was too poor to buy me clothes that fit. And then laughed about it."

There was silence as they absorbed this, and Leo suddenly felt sick to his stomach. That couldn't be true—could it?

"He did not," Leo said weakly. "I mean, I know he made fun of your jeans but—"

"He made fun of my jeans *and* my mom," Nicky said, typing as he spoke, as if this conversation was no big deal. But Leo could hear the intensity in his voice and suspected this mattered to him—a lot. "And yes, at that time my mom was too poor to get me jeans that fit, and yes, I was angry about it, so yes, I spray-painted his hockey gear." He looked up and locked eyes with Olivia. "I'm sorry for some of the things I did, but not that. That I'd do again in a heartbeat."

Leo had to admit he could kind of see his point—*if* Steve had really said that.

"Yasmin didn't do anything to you," Olivia said, voice barbed.

Nicky rubbed his forehead for a moment. "Yeah, I know, I just—I'm sorry about that."

Olivia snorted. "Even if that's true, that doesn't help anything. She's gone."

Leo winced at the sadness in Olivia's voice.

"If there is something else I can do, I'll do it," Nicky said, brushing his hair from his face. "I swear. I'll apologize to other people too. And some of what I did to other people, I can fix, at least a little." Leo was unsure what to believe. Nicky seemed sincere but what if this whole thing was some kind of long con?

"If you regret it, why did you do it all in the first place?" Gracie asked. She sounded more curious than angry.

Nicky let out a breath and was silent so long Leo wasn't sure he was ever going to answer. He could hear birds calling, scuffles of small animals in the trees outside, the faint burbling of the creek. He had a moment of wondering if some of the scuffling might be a small bear or a loud snake but then Olivia spoke.

"That must have been hard, when your mom didn't have enough money to buy you jeans that fit." She sounded almost as surprised as Leo that she, of all people, had offered this understanding to Nicky.

Nicky shrugged and twisted the cord of his laptop. "Yeah, and she wasn't around a lot and sometimes we didn't have food and the electricity went off a few times. It was—well, it wasn't good."

It was hard for Leo to wrap his brain around what this would be like. Food and his parents always being around were a given, something that just was. Like electricity. What if it was winter and the electricity went off? Did it impact the heat too? Would Nicky have been cold? Winters in Snow Valley were freezing. Could you still cook or did the gas go off too? Though if you didn't have enough food, then there wasn't anything to cook, so maybe that part wasn't a problem. But the not-enough-food was a huge problem. You could get sick if it went on too long. And pretty much everyone Leo knew was unpleasant when hungry—and for Leo that was just because he'd biked too long and forgotten a snack. What if you actually didn't have dinner? Or breakfast? You'd probably be—well, you'd probably be extremely short-tempered, like Nicky. And while Leo complained his parents got over-involved in his life, he wasn't dumb enough to think he didn't need them around. What if something bad happened, like the time Leo somehow jammed the bathtub faucet and flooded the bathroom? It had been rough (and his parents had had a great deal to say about Leo's choices) but if Mom hadn't been there and known exactly what to do, the whole house could have been destroyed. Plus if your parents weren't around, who made sure you had what you needed for school and made sure you got up on time and took you to the dentist even when you didn't want to go? It would be scary, scarier than Leo could fully understand.

"I know it sounds like an excuse," Nicky went on, the words running together, "but everything going on, it made me angry, like, all the time. For those two years I was never *not* angry. So anytime anyone looked at me wrong, I just kind of lost it."

It was not hard to understand that. It was really easy for Leo to lash out at people when he was angry—that was why his parents were so big on "taking a breathing break when you have big feelings." Because sometimes those feelings made you say things you didn't think or mean. Once it passed, you could find the right words to say what you really felt and meant. But if you were always angry, how could you breathe and find those words?

"I mean, sometimes people had it coming, like your friend Steve or Jessica when she told everyone my mom got fired from her dad's bank for being a bad worker."

"Did she get fired?" Leo asked, suddenly imagining a whole new side to the story.

"Why is it your business or anyone else's?" Nicky snapped as both Olivia and Gracie shot sharp looks at Leo.

Oh, good point. "Sorry," Leo mumbled. It *wasn't* his business—or Jessica's. And Jessica shouldn't have told everyone—that was mean. Though Nicky's infamous solution of gum in her hair wasn't exactly nice either.

Gracie was apparently satisfied by Leo's response

because she turned back to Nicky and moved on. "You told us things are better now," she said.

Nicky nodded. "Yeah."

"What changed?" Leo asked bluntly. He had a second of worrying he'd yet again put his foot in his mouth but this time no one snapped or glared.

Nicky just took a moment to gaze at each of them, his eyes challenging. "My neighbor called the Child Welfare Office finally, and it took awhile but my mom got help and got better. We have a social worker and my mom has a job and, yeah, we're good." He smiled, seemingly despite himself. "Really good." Then his eyes narrowed at Leo, his freckles standing out on his suddenly pale cheeks. "But if I hear about this from your friend Steve, I'll know where it came from."

That stung.

"You won't hear about it from Steve and it's not because you threatened me," Leo said, looking right back at Nicky. "It's because your mom getting better isn't a joke. It's actually really cool."

Nicky gazed at Leo for a moment and Leo realized it was the first time Nicky had seemed to really look at him, not just sneer as his eyes slipped over Leo.

Leo held Nicky's gaze and also for the first time really looked at Nicky, the circles under his eyes, the eyes that looked older than a twelve-year-old boy's, which held feelings Leo wasn't sure he'd ever known.

Nicky nodded once, then went back to his computer. Leo felt as if he'd passed a test, a test that he hadn't realized mattered to him until this very second. He often felt tested when he was with the guys because he needed to prove he was one of them—but this was different. It wasn't about proving something to Nicky—it was about who Leo was.

Gracie gave Leo an approving nod while Olivia flashed him a thumbs-up. Two more tests passed that mattered to him.

But then something else occurred to him. "She must be really worried about you—your mom, I mean."

Nicky gave him a look of disdain. "Obviously I texted her and told her I'm fine."

"But doesn't she want to know where you are?" Leo asked, imagining how furious his mom would be if he ever pulled something like this.

"I mean, yeah, but the important thing is she knows I'm safe," he said, shrugging. "And she'll be a lot more worried if I can't figure out a way out of this hacking thing." His voice was heavy on the last few words.

Gracie cleared her throat. "Have you made any progress with that?

"No," Nicky said, his whole body sagging with the admission.

"Okay, well, let us see what we can find out," Gracie said.

"Um, we're not computer experts," Leo pointed out.

Gracie laughed. "No, not what we can find out about the email, what we can find out about the person who sent it and set the whole thing up. A new investigation."

Nicky inhaled sharply at her words. "Seriously?" he asked, his voice light with surprise and a hint of wonder. "You'd really help me?"

"We discovered you, so we can help find the mastermind behind this," Leo said rather heroically because Nicky was looking at them (well, the girls anyway) like they were superhuman.

"*If*," Olivia added, "you start apologizing and fixing things. Right now, before we even leave. And you start with Yasmin."

Nicky hesitated and the cabin was silent. Then he looked up.

"No," he said.

"Then—" Olivia began, voice loud.

But Nicky spoke over her.

"I'm starting with you, Olivia," he said. "I'm sorry that what I did made your friend leave." He took a deep breath. "I'm really, really sorry."

CHAPTER 13

GRACIE

The three nearly ran back to their bikes. "We're going to talk to Ryan, right?" Gracie asked, because he was the one she'd thought of when they agreed to get help for Nicky. If Ryan didn't know who was responsible, he was the best person to figure it out with them.

"Yup," Olivia confirmed, sidestepping an old puddle that was more muck than water.

"Ryan's not secretly the hacker or anything?" Leo asked. "I mean, what if he got all these people to help him with the list but the whole time he was using it to get information so he could frame Nicky?"

Normally Gracie would have found that more like a comic book plot than real life, but the past half hour now made her wonder if maybe comics were based on real life. "He did make a big thing about not knowing tech stuff," Gracie remembered. "What if that was just a front?"

"No, it's true," Olivia said. "You guys are right to be careful because we have no idea who's behind this so it could be anyone. But Mr. Simmons had an after-school group for people who needed extra help in tech class—it was Yasmin, Gus, Ilana, and Ryan, and since they're neighbors, Yasmin and Ryan walked home together a lot. That's also how he knew to ask her to help add to the list. So don't worry, he's safe. He wanted to expose all the bad things Nicky did but I don't think he'd try to get Nicky in trouble for something he hadn't done."

That was reassuring.

They clambered onto their bikes and headed back to Snow Valley. Gracie was pumped up and took an early lead, the physicality of biking fast a satisfying release after the tension of the past hours.

"We're doing the right thing, right?" Leo asked, puffing slightly as he caught up to her on Kappa Path. She realized he was struggling to keep up and that Olivia was several paces behind them so she slowed a bit.

"I mean," he went on, "Nicky did awful stuff to people and maybe he does have this coming. I got all swept up in the moment when we were going to be heroes and save Nicky, but now I'm not sure we're on the right side."

Gracie considered as she maneuvered her bike around a turtle in the path. "Yeah, he did," she said. "But does that make it okay to do it back to him? I mean, it's like you get bullied and then what? It's okay for you to bully back?"

"That's a good point," Leo agreed. "And he is sorry—that's worth something."

Olivia had caught up to them and pulled up on Gracie's other side. "I hate to say it but I agree," she admitted. "I started this day determined to see Nicky go down but now that doesn't seem as important anymore. I'm not going to lie, it meant something to me when he apologized."

Gracie bit back a smile. It had clearly meant something to Olivia when Nicky apologized—it had meant a lot, at least if her reaction of excessive blinking, pink cheeks, and bright eyes was any indication. Not to mention the way she carefully put Nicky's number into her phone and promised to text him with any news.

"It meant more than seeing him suffer the consequences, if that makes sense," Olivia went on as they coasted down a small hill. They'd be on Main Street in just a few minutes.

"Yeah, isn't that *why* you want someone to face consequences?" Gracie asked. The smell of the woods—autumn leaves, pine needles, the freshness of the creek—was now mixing with town smells of fireplaces, car exhaust, and mowed grass. "So they regret what they did and they're sorry? Nicky already feels that way so why would he need to be punished? What would it accomplish?"

"Nothing," Leo said after having thought it through. "That's a good point. You guys are right—it wouldn't accomplish anything."

"Nope," Olivia agreed. "It could even make things worse."

"So now we're Team Nicky," Leo said, sounding reassured.

They reached the end of the path and turned left onto Main Street, which was houses for the next few blocks and then the start of downtown. And that meant they had time to talk about the thing that had started nagging at Gracie as soon as they got on their bikes back at the campground.

"There's something I'm worried about," Gracie said. "The police are still out there looking for Nicky—shouldn't we let them know he's safe?"

Olivia spoke up immediately. "We told Nicky we wouldn't—we can't go back on that."

Gracie would have been amused at how quick Olivia was to defend Nicky—it was such a change from the morning—but she was too focused on her concerns that keeping Nicky's secret was a bad call. Didn't they have some kind of citizen obligation to report him?

"But what if we're breaking a law by not saying anything? And the longer this goes on, the worse it probably is for Ms. Becker," Gracie said. Her hands ached and she realized it was because she was gripping her handlebars so tightly. "And it's not like we made a promise to Nicky not to tell anyone. We just said we hadn't done it *yet*."

"I don't think it's breaking the law," Leo said. "If the police ask us, we have to tell the truth, of course, but they don't have any reason to talk to us now."

Gracie's brain instantly went back to the morning, when the police had had reason to talk to them, and her chest squeezed up like it had then. Talking to the police was scary, even though they'd been nice to her.

"If we call the police before figuring out how to help Nicky prove his innocence, he has no reason to keep his promise to us to apologize to people and make things right. He might even retaliate against us," Olivia said.

Hmm, Gracie had not considered that.

"Yeah, Nicky may be nicer now but I wouldn't mess with him—he said not to call the police and we need to respect that," Leo said.

They slowed as they arrived at one of Main Street's three traffic lights, which was currently red, and came to a stop.

"But you're right about Ms. Becker and probably other people at the school too," Olivia said. "How about this? We take two hours to see if we can stop whoever is setting Nicky up, and then go to the police."

Gracie let out a breath, her fingers now loosening to a normal grip on her bike handles, because that sounded good.

"But we'll go earlier if we find the spear phisher

before that," Olivia added. "And obviously we'll let Nicky know when we do."

Gracie and Leo exchanged a smirk at Olivia's new loyalty to Nicky, and then Gracie nodded, helmet bobbing.

"Okay," she agreed.

The light turned green, and after checking for any cars speeding through the intersection (a biking rule her parents had drilled into her), Gracie led the way to the library. A few minutes later they'd arrived, parked their bikes, and were trooping to the back computers, where Ryan appeared to be exactly where he'd been when they found him this morning. Which felt like days ago to Gracie.

"Hey, so we—" Olivia began when they'd reached him, but Ryan held up a silencing hand.

"Not here," he said.

"No, it's okay, Nicky isn't spying on us," Olivia said, sitting down on the wooden chair next to Ryan.

"You can't know that," Ryan said, the corners of his mouth tightening.

"We do," Gracie said, leaning back against the computer table.

"Because we know where he is," Leo added eagerly,

hovering between Gracie and Olivia and bouncing a bit on his toes.

Ryan let out a loud breath. "Excellent! So the police have him."

"No," Leo said, looking alarmed. "He's still hiding but he's not near here. So he can't overhear us."

Gracie would have laughed at how befuddled Leo was but the stakes were too high and the clock was ticking. "Listen, the point is that Nicky isn't the problem anymore."

Ryan was clearly baffled. "What?"

"We found out someone is trying to frame him for a crime he didn't commit," Leo jumped in.

Gracie raised a brow at him and he ducked his head, hopefully ready to keep a lid on his rambling.

"Someone is setting him up," Olivia explained. "Framing him for trying to hack into the school computers, and if they aren't stopped, Nicky will be in real trouble."

Ryan looked at her blankly. "So what's the problem with that?"

Gracie sucked in her breath. This was not the reaction she'd expected.

"The problem is that he didn't do it," she told Ryan.

"Whatever," Ryan said, going back to his typing.

"Wait up," Olivia said sharply. "I thought your plan was to expose things Nicky had done—make him face consequences for how he hurt people. Not frame him for things he never did."

"Clearly someone else has different ideas," Ryan said with a shrug. "And that's not my problem."

"You're okay with it?" Gracie asked, disbelieving.

Ryan's blue eyes met her gaze and he shrugged again. "Why not? Nicky did all kinds of awful stuff. If someone wants a little extra revenge, why would it bother me?"

Olivia leaned forward fast and snakelike, making Ryan recoil. Gracie felt a flash of pride—no one messed with Olivia. "Because it's bullying Nicky and that's not okay."

"But he bullied half the school," Ryan protested.

"So Nicky being a bully makes it fine for everyone to bully him? It's doing exactly what people hated having done to them, so how is it okay for them to do it to someone else? Is there a bullying pass you can get that makes it acceptable for some people but not others?" Olivia was right in Ryan's face now, clearly on a roll.

"I guess I never thought about it that way," Ryan said slowly.

"Clearly not," Olivia said self-righteously, which made Gracie bite back a grin because less than an hour ago Olivia would have agreed with Ryan. But they'd learned quite a few things in the past hour—things that had changed their minds about a lot—and that would hopefully help them change other people's minds as well.

"Either you're okay with bullying or you're not," Leo said, folding his arms over his chest.

"I'm not, obviously," Ryan said, now starting to look confused.

"Great, then you can start helping us figure out who's doing this to Nicky," Olivia said cheerfully.

"Oh, but I—" Ryan began, then faltered.

"Listen, what Nicky did to you and everyone else on that list you're making—it's not okay," Gracie said, pressing her palms together. "But it's also complicated—there's more to the story. And none of us ever bothered to find that out until the three of us discovered him today. Yes, Nicky needs to try and fix things and face consequences for what he did. But that's happening anyway, even without you publishing all the info you've gathered."

"What?" Ryan asked, brows now crinkling up.

"He's reaching out to people as we speak, making amends," Leo said. "Just wait—yours is coming."

"And the thing is," Gracie said, standing straight now because what she had to say was important to her. "That's what we want—Nicky to be sorry and try to make up for what he did. We don't need him to suffer punishment for something he never even did—that serves no one."

"And it just continues the cycle of bullying," Olivia finished.

Ryan nodded, his eyes focused on a point behind Gracie—clearly he was weighing their words.

"Okay, yeah, I see that," he said finally. "You're right—it's not cool to frame him. But I really don't know who's behind it."

Gracie saw Olivia's shoulders sag and Leo sighed. "Do you have any guesses?" she asked.

Ryan rubbed his chin. "Not really. But it has to be someone who's good at tech stuff, right? So maybe it's one of the kids on the tech team that's working on posting the list on Socially Safe. Maybe someone decided it wasn't enough and they wanted to take things further."

Olivia was sitting up again and Leo was once again bouncing on his toes.

"Who's on the team?" Olivia asked.

"Abby, Jordan, Jessica, Bryce, Aiyana, and Joe," Ryan said. "That's it—we kept the group small so word wouldn't spread. Oh, except once they asked Ben, the president of the high school computer club, about something. But I don't know how much they told him, and if he really knew what they were up to. Ben probably didn't care what a group of middle schoolers was doing."

Ryan waved at someone behind them and Gracie turned—it was Chloe. Her pale skin was blotchy and red—clearly she'd been crying.

"Hey," she said, sitting down next to Ryan and giving an attempt at a smile to Olivia, Gracie, and Leo, who all said hi back.

"How's it going?" Ryan asked.

Chloe shrugged.

If they could fix the mess with Nicky's hacker today, maybe Ms. Becker would keep her job and Chloe wouldn't have to move.

"See you later," Gracie said to both Ryan and Chloe as they headed out. Gracie was now extra motivated to find the person framing Nicky.

"So who do we talk to first?" Olivia asked once they were back outside in the sun in front of the library. "I think—"

"No," Leo interrupted.

Olivia turned to him with a sour expression. "So what's your brilliant idea?" she asked, hands on hips.

"We eat," Leo announced. "We eat immediately."

CHAPTER 14

OLIVIA

"I *was* hungry," Olivia admitted after inhaling half her slice of pepperoni pizza from Chester's Cheesy Pizza. Their first choice had been Batter Up for doughnuts but the line was too long. There was no wait for pizza, though, and as they walked down the sidewalk eating, Olivia could not imagine anything better.

Leo made some kind of sound through his mouthful of food that Olivia assumed either meant "me too" or "I told you we needed to stop and eat something."

"No talking with food in your mouth," Olivia scolded. "We've already been over this."

She saw Leo roll his eyes but he didn't bother responding once he swallowed—he just took another big bite of pizza loaded with sausage and mushrooms. Olivia got that—the toppings at Chester's were luscious.

They'd decided to talk to Abby first since she was

closest. As they stopped for the red light on the corner, Olivia eyed Gracie, who'd opted for plain cheese—definitely a missed opportunity. Though maybe it had to do with Gracie's overactive sense of smell.

"You should become a detective," she told Gracie, who choked a little as she swallowed, as if this had come out of the blue. So Olivia explained as the light turned green and they crossed Gingerbread Lane to the other side of Main Street.

"It was your nose that found Nicky—without your nasal superpowers we'd still be looking for him."

Leo snorted. "Nasal superpowers—good one."

Gracie's eyes narrowed slightly and her mouth tightened. "I don't care for it," she informed him.

He raised a hand in surrender and went back to his pizza. Olivia had to admit Gracie had impressed her today: She was no quiet bunny, not anymore anyway.

"Thank you, I think," Gracie said to Olivia. "Usually my super-charged smelling ability is just a pain but it did help us today." She turned to Leo. "You can call it super-charged."

Leo started to speak with his mouth full, then looked at Olivia and just gave Gracie a thumbs-up.

Olivia swallowed her last bite, then wiped her hands on her napkin and glanced around for a garbage can. There was one in front of the karate school and she headed over, Gracie with her own napkin next to her. It was only after they'd started back down the sidewalk that she noticed Leo wasn't with them. She turned and saw that he was standing a few feet back, glowering at something across the street.

"What's up?" Olivia asked as she and Gracie walked back to him.

"I think I saw Gus," Leo said darkly.

"So what?" Olivia asked.

Gracie peered across the street. "I don't see him."

Olivia looked, still not getting why it mattered, and saw only a group of sixth graders in front of her family's comic book store and a dad pushing a stroller. Chloe was on the corner, probably heading back home, and a group of eighth graders including Nora from the paper and Maddie, one of the members of the dance team, were walking out of Batter Up. But no Gus.

"He was there," Leo said, scowling but finally starting toward Abby's house.

"And that matters because . . . ?" Olivia asked, noticing that her voice lacked bite. Talking to Gracie and Leo about Benji had loosened something inside her, making it easier to breathe, and then Nicky's apology—and genuine regret over hurting both her and Yasmin—had softened it even more. She felt lighter, more mellowed out, but was this a good thing? Olivia certainly didn't want to lose her edge—that was how she got things done, after all.

"I'm telling you, he's been following us," Leo said, his face pinched.

"Why would he do that?" Gracie asked.

Olivia thought this was an excellent question.

"I bet he's the one who framed Nicky, so he's tailing us to make sure we don't find the clues we need to prove it," Leo said.

Olivia snorted. "I highly doubt that," she said. "He doesn't have the computer skills to frame anyone."

It was obvious to Olivia this hadn't occurred to Leo. "Maybe he thought we'd lead him to Nicky," he guessed, sounding less confident.

"Then where was he when we found Nicky?" Olivia pointed out.

"Fine, I don't know why," he said, sounding slightly sulky. "But he definitely is."

"Whatever," Olivia said, voice stern but feeling pleased: Leo's quick acquiescence to her argument had assured her that her edge was still there. But then something else occurred to her. "But you know who might be tracking us is Chloe."

"For real?" Leo asked.

"Yeah," Olivia said. "I mean, she showed up when we were in the library with Ryan and I just saw her a minute ago too. If Ryan told her what we were doing and she had reason to stop us, following us would be the logical thing to do." Now *that* was a reason to tail someone, unlike Leo's random theories about Gus.

"So she didn't even stay at the library long," Leo mused. "Do you see her now?"

They all glanced around but there was no sign of Chloe.

"Is she a realistic suspect?" Gracie asked as the three of them moved around a slow stroller on the sidewalk. "Like, she hasn't been here that long—would she have reason to get Nicky in trouble after only knowing him a few weeks?"

"He's been known to make quick enemies," Leo pointed out. But then his brows squinched up. "But not this year so, no, I don't think so. Plus she doesn't even have a phone, so how into tech stuff is she?"

That was an excellent point and Olivia mentally crossed Chloe off the suspect list.

They'd reached the building where Abby's family lived, on the second floor above the sporting goods store they owned. Abby and her brother usually helped out on weekends and after school, and sure enough when they looked in the big window, Olivia saw Abby straightening a display of winter hats at the front of the store.

Gracie pushed open the doors, Leo and Olivia right behind. When Abby saw them she hurried their way. "Mom, I'll be back in a minute," she called, waving them back outside.

"You guys!" she exclaimed when they were on the sidewalk. "Ryan texted me. I can't believe someone is trying to blackmail Nicky!"

"Frame him, not blackmail him," Olivia corrected quickly.

"Right, sorry, that's what I meant," Abby said,

laughing. "I'm losing it because the most incredible thing just happened: Nicky texted me to apologize for calling me a—well, calling me a really rude name and pushing me and making my phone fall out of my bag. He even offered to help pay for it if it broke but I just needed a new screen protector so it was no big deal. But him offering—it was really cool."

Olivia realized she was grinning proudly though wasn't exactly sure why. Was it possible she was actually feeling pride in *Nicky*, the boy who'd been her sworn enemy for so long?

"So yeah, but about the framing thing—we can't let it happen, it's awful!" Abby went on, her sunny glow disappearing as she frowned deeply. "Who do you guys think is behind it?"

Olivia tried not to react to this extremely disappointing question, especially after Leo sighed loudly. "We were hoping you'd have an idea," she told Abby, not mentioning that Abby herself had been their current suspect.

"No," Abby said, her eyes clouding with sadness. "I wish I did but I can't imagine who would do such a thing." Olivia'd had a lot of classes with Abby and was familiar with her dramatic ways and tendency to chatter. Olivia usually enjoyed it but not today.

"Okay, well, I guess we'll try someone else," Leo said, inching away from Abby and giving Olivia a "let's get going" head tilt.

"I'd go with you," Abby said, her voice now determined as Leo's eyes widened and Gracie looked panicked at the thought of Abby joining them, "but I have another mission. I'm going to stop the post from going up on Socially Safe. Nicky is sorry for his past mistakes and ready to begin reparations and we need to support that, not shame him on social media. I mean, he—"

"Great, thanks," Olivia said, cutting Abby off before she could get going on a monologue. And preventing the Socially Safe post *was* a good idea—Olivia hadn't been thinking about it, since the phishing thing was so much worse, but it would be shaming to Nicky to have his past displayed and, as Abby had said, it was no longer necessary.

Gracie and Leo headed down the sidewalk and Olivia followed, trying to decide which tech team member they should speak with next. Aiyana was always standing up for causes she believed in and was probably the most honest person in the grade, so it couldn't be her. Jessica wasn't a rule breaker; Joe was a follower, not a leader; Jordan was too sweet to consider something so underhanded; and Bryce wasn't vindictive enough. Was it possible the phisher was someone else? Or did one of the team members have a shady side Olivia had never seen? They *were* planning to post on Socially Safe in a way that wasn't entirely aboveboard—so that had her back to thinking it could be any of them . . .

"I wonder if there's anyone else we should consider as a suspect" she said, thinking out loud and coming to a stop. "I mean, maybe someone on the tech team talked to someone and—"

She had more to say but Leo interrupted.

"Of course!" he nearly shouted, starting down the sidewalk before the girls had even agreed. "We're finding Ben!"

"I don't know," Olivia said. "I'm not seeing it. He's a high schooler. What could he possibly have against Nicky? Even if he helped the tech team out with something, he probably didn't even know what they were up to."

Gracie tilted her head to the side. "I agree with Olivia. Why do you think we should talk to Ben?" she asked.

"Because," Leo said, his eyes bright as he bounced on his toes, "I know who's framing Nicky and Ben is the key!"

CHAPTER 15

LEO

What Leo couldn't believe was that it had taken him this long to figure it out! The answer had been in front of them all day. Or, to be completely accurate, behind them.

"So who is it?" Olivia demanded. Leo was tempted to drag out the delicious moment but it was too thrilling to keep to himself—plus they still had to stop the scheme from happening.

"It's Gus," Leo announced, spreading out his hands. "That's why he's been tailing us all day."

Gracie's forehead crinkled up. "Gus isn't a tech guy. He's always messing up coding projects because he wants to finish and sneak onto YouTube, and those are pretty simple. He doesn't know the basics, let alone how to hack."

Olivia was nodding.

"But Ben does," Leo said, smiling wide.

Olivia scowled. "So?"

185

"So," Leo crowed, "Ben is Gus's older brother!"

"Oooh," Gracie said as Olivia grinned and reached out to high-five Leo. Leo slapped her hand with gusto because it had been pretty brilliant on his part.

"Didn't you see Gus by Batter Up?" Gracie asked. "Why don't we just find him?"

"Yeah, but we don't know where he is now and I happen to know Ben has karate in ten minutes so he's easiest to find," Leo said. He did not add that he knew this because he had briefly been in the white belt class before Ben's red belt group but had been asked to move to the elementary class because he needed "more time working on fundamentals." He'd quit immediately, humiliated just picturing what would happen if Steve and the guys knew he practiced karate with seven-year-olds. He did miss karate though—he'd felt strong slicing through the air and kicking the hanging sandbag, which made a very satisfying thunk if you whacked it hard enough.

"You guys!" It was Abby, rushing up to them and beaming. "I called a meeting and the whole tech team is coming!"

"You got them to stop the Socially Safe posting?"

Leo asked, surprised it had been so easy to convince everyone.

"Oh, no, I just got everyone to agree to meet at the library," Abby clarified. "I told them we have something vital to discuss. Ryan will be there too, of course, since this whole thing was his idea."

"That's really—" Gracie began but Abby cut her off.

"Sorry, gotta go, it's starting in ten minutes!" And with that Abby was off, skirting around a tourist family with a large stroller and jogging across the street the moment the light turned green.

"I'm glad she's doing that," Gracie said, watching her go and then starting down the sidewalk toward Kenshikai Karate.

"Same," Olivia agreed. They made their way past a slew of people streaming out of the movie theater. The Snow Valley Cinema had a single theater, which showed old movies from the eighties and nineties, charged three dollars for tickets, and was always packed. Olivia waved to the Stevenson-Millers, an elderly couple who often had neighbors over for barbecues in the summer and cheese fondue in the winter.

Leo was concerned that his moment of glory had

been cut short by Abby. "Pretty amazing how I figured out the phisher," he reminded the girls.

Olivia snickered, which was exasperating, but Gracie patted his arm and said "Good job" in a condescending manner, which was worse. He was about to point out that he, like Gracie, would be a terrific detective, when Ben turned the corner, nearly plowing into them.

"Hey, we were looking for you!" Leo said.

"I can't help," Ben said, smoothly sidestepping them and continuing down the sidewalk.

Olivia gave Leo and Gracie an outraged look, then charged after him. "Um, you don't know that," she said, planting herself firmly in front of him. "We didn't even tell you what we need."

"Right, what I should have said is that I don't want to help so I won't," Ben said snippily. "I'm on my way to karate."

Wow, no wonder Gus was a jerk, with this guy as an older brother.

"We know what you and Gus did," Gracie told Ben coolly, stepping up next to Olivia as Ben tried to slither by.

"Yeah," Leo added, coming to Olivia's other side.

"I don't know what that punk did, but I didn't help him do it," Ben said. "Take it up with him. He's right there." He pointed across the street, and when they turned to look, Ben charged past them.

Leo would have tried to stop him, or at least gesture to Olivia to try and stop him, but given how difficult Ben was, they were better off just confronting Gus.

"I told you he was following us!" Leo crowed.

"Yeah, and now we know why," Olivia said, starting toward the crosswalk. But then she paused and grinned at him. "He and Ben hacked Nicky, and Gus has been trying to make sure we don't figure it out. You were right, I admit it."

With almost anyone else Leo would have gloated, but he was too pleased by Olivia's acknowledgment to do anything but beam as a frothy sweetness spread through him.

The light changed in their favor as they reached the corner, and Leo walked in front as they marched over to Gus. Unfortunately at the last minute Leo caught his toe on an especially wide space between sidewalk squares and tripped, nearly falling before managing to regain his balance. It was also possible he'd let out a small shriek.

"Smooth," Gus scoffed as Leo's face began to heat up. "You're such a wimp."

Leo's insides curdled in shame.

"Watch it," Gracie said sharply. She took a step toward Gus, and to Leo's surprise, her tall stance actually looked rather intimidating.

"So now you need girls to defend you?" Gus asked, though Leo noticed he took a step back.

"Why would that be a problem?" Olivia asked, her voice chilly.

"Oh yeah, no, it's not," Gus said quickly, taking another step back and nearly crashing into a tourist couple. "Sorry," he said, turning to them. His cheeks were turning red and all of a sudden Leo wasn't ashamed. Or angry at Gus. In fact, he felt bad for him. Because Gus was just doing what Leo had always done: try to prove he was like Steve.

And that was when Leo realized something: Gus was not the phisher after all. Why would he be? He was too busy trying to impress Steve to care about Nicky. Kind of like Leo. Actually, exactly like Leo, at least until today. Leo let out a small sigh of disappointment as he realized they still were no closer to figuring out who was phishing.

But then if Gus didn't care about Nicky, there was still the mystery of why he'd been trailing them all day. What could he possibly want from them? And then Leo realized what he himself had once had that *would* impress Steve.

"You've been following us all day . . ." Leo said to Gus, who began to say something, but Leo spoke over him. ". . . because you want to return my knife."

"What?" Olivia said.

Leo was watching Gus, and he saw him sag a bit as the bluster slipped out of him. "I wasn't following you *all* day—I live at Cassidy," he said. "So I just happened to see you guys there. But I did try to find you a few times to give it back. I was going to leave it on your bike but you're always dropping it so I worried the knife would fall off."

Olivia stifled a laugh at this.

"Anyway, yeah, I took it," he said, handing it back, carefully sheathed in its case, and not quite looking Leo in the eye.

"You wanted me to look stupid in front of Steve when I didn't have the knife to show everyone," Leo guessed.

Gus squinted, his gaze focused somewhere off in the distance. Leo knew this meant he had guessed correctly.

There were a lot of things Leo could've said right then, threatening Gus or shaming him back. But Leo knew he had only one true response.

"Thanks," he said. "I'm really glad to have it back. I was stupid to take it from my brother in the first place."

Gus stared at Leo for a moment as the girls stepped away, letting Leo take it from here.

"Not as stupid as I was to take it from your backpack," Gus said, shaking his head. "Ms. Becker almost caught me sneaking out of the cabin before lights out and I had to make up this whole thing about how I thought Nicky had my backpack by mistake. Then she almost woke Nicky up and then I would have been in real trouble."

Leo laughed and after a moment Gus joined in. The sun was shining on Leo's face but the warmth came from inside him because he liked laughing with Gus. And hanging out with Olivia and Gracie. He hadn't felt this much like—well, like himself in a long time. Maybe because instead of trying to be the kind of guy Steve approved of he was just being Leo.

Gus glanced down at the knife Leo was tucking carefully in his pocket. "I'm going to meet Steve and the guys if you want to come and show it to them now."

It was generous of Gus to offer because if Leo went he'd have the limelight, all of Steve's attention and admiration, because he would have the knife. It would prove that Leo belonged.

But for the first time Leo was questioning what kind of guy he *actually* wanted to be. He'd been striving to fit in with Steve and the others without ever considering the way they were tough. Because in truth there were lots of ways to be tough. Like Olivia—her assertiveness and her confidence were pretty great. She used them to speak up for herself and for things she believed in. Or Gracie, who had become impressively outspoken and honest over the day—she wasn't just tough, she was powerful. But neither Olivia nor Gracie ever used their toughness to make other people feel small, the way Steve did.

What Nicky said back in Cobra had shaken Leo:

Steve mocking Nicky's family for having money struggles wasn't tough—it was mean. And it had Leo remembering other times that Steve had said or done things that hadn't quite felt okay, things they'd all chalked up to Steve being a tough, bold leader. But maybe that wasn't leadership at all. Maybe all this time Leo had mistaken Steve's brand of tough for strength when in fact it was more like bullying. And acting like Steve, trying to be part of his inside crew, had inspired Leo to take Noah's knife. He'd risked hurting his brother, risked getting in serious trouble bringing a knife on a school trip, for what? For the approval of a guy so callous he'd mock Nicky's hardship?

What had Leo been thinking?

"Leo, we should get going," Gracie called from where she and Olivia were waiting in front of Snowy Day Books and Treasures, a store Leo had avoided because Steve called it the place for nerds.

A store Leo would now be going to whenever he wanted.

Gus looked at him. "You coming?" he asked.

"No, thanks," Leo said. And he headed back to his friends.

CHAPTER 16

GRACIE

Gracie sighed as Gus turned the corner and vanished from sight: another lead that led nowhere. The clock was ticking and they *had* to help Nicky. "Okay," she said, looking at Olivia and Leo, "I say we head to the library for Abby's meeting of the tech team to see if one of them might have done it."

"Agreed," Olivia said, walking down the block toward the library so fast she was almost running.

"What do we do when we get there?" Leo asked, hurrying to keep up. "Question them?"

Gracie's hair blew into her face, momentarily blinding her. She swept it back irritably, stumbling slightly as she struggled to tighten her ponytail.

"I think we start by announcing that we uncovered the plot to frame Nicky and then read the room," Olivia said.

"What does that mean?" Gracie asked, though she

saw Leo was nodding—it was probably a comic book thing.

"We see how people react," Leo said. "Who looks surprised, who asks questions—"

"And most importantly," Olivia interrupted, "who looks guilty."

"Oh, got it," Gracie said. "That sounds good."

They'd reached the intersection and stopped as the light changed to red. The sun was low in the sky, giving the trees in front of the library long shadows. Which meant it was getting late—they were running out of time.

"We know it's not Abby so who else could it be?" Gracie said, thinking if they could come up with the most likely suspects they'd have a better chance reading the room.

"I can't picture Joe doing anything mean like hacking someone, but Nicky did get him suspended from the hockey team for a week last year," Leo offered.

"Why, what did Joe do to Nicky?" Olivia asked. She was shifting her weight from side to side, clearly impatient for the green light so they could get going.

Leo shrugged. "I'm not sure," he said. "But it makes

him a possible suspect, I guess—he was super upset about it—he missed a game and everything."

Gracie nodded as another gust of wind hit them. "We can see what he does when we tell them about the hack," she said. "Anyone else?" It was kind of frustrating that she had so little knowledge of her classmates. She'd spent so much time with Mina that only the biggest gossip made it into her orbit.

"Bryce was really angry when Nicky ruined his art project right before the spring festival," Olivia said. "He's so nice, it's hard to imagine him being devious and hacking, but maybe he was just that angry."

"So we keep an eye on him too," Leo said as the light finally changed and they hustled across.

Gracie was realizing something unfortunate: Between her aggressive hair and the fact that she'd drunk too much water when they were waiting for their slices at Chester's, she was going to need a pit stop.

They reached the top of the steps but could not get in: Apparently toddler story hour had just finished so a parade of strollers and little kids holding their caregivers' hands was clogging the entryway as they headed, rather loudly, out. Gracie tried not to laugh when a small boy shouting "More books!" barreled into Olivia's legs, causing her to leap backward.

Once the doorway had cleared, they slipped through. Ms. MacCullough was kneeling down with several toddlers who were reluctant to leave, but Lucy, one of the assistant librarians, was behind the desk and she smiled at them. "Looking for your friends?" she asked. "They went to conference room one."

"Thanks," Olivia said, starting toward the room, but Gracie caught her elbow.

"I'll catch up with you guys," she said. "I need the bathroom." She turned left and half ran to the ladies' room. After peeing and washing her hands, she pulled her hair free of the now snarled ponytail and began to speedily twist it into a braid.

The door to the bathroom swung open and Jessica walked in. "Hey," she said, catching sight of Gracie in front of the mirror.

"Hi," Gracie said, the greeting muffled by the hair band she held in her mouth.

"You have such pretty hair," Jessica said, her intense gaze focused on Gracie in the mirror.

"Thanks," Gracie said absently. She took the band

from her mouth and wrapped it around the end of the braid, then waved goodbye to Jessica and rushed back out to rejoin her friends.

"You took forever," Leo said the moment Gracie emerged. He and Olivia, who had been waiting right outside the ladies' room, came up on either side of her as Olivia scolded him.

"It's never okay to say that to someone coming out of the bathroom," Olivia said as they made their way to conference room one. "What if Gracie had digestive issues?"

"I did not have digestive issues, thank you very much," Gracie said, amused to see how the phrase made Leo crack up. "But I had to get my hair out of my face—it was driving me bananas."

"You should just cut it off," Leo said.

The words caused something to flicker just on the edge of Gracie's thoughts, but there was no time to figure it out as they rushed across the library.

Conference room one had a large table surrounded by wooden chairs and was decorated with book posters and a big bulletin board with flyers of upcoming programs. Gracie was a regular at things like Afternoon of Crafting and Book Tasting Tuesdays, though the video game tournaments and poetry slams got the biggest turnout from the middle school. Abby stood at the head of the table, Ryan beside her, the rest of the tech team sitting down.

". . . really think we shouldn't," Abby said, apparently winding down a long monologue, if the zombie-fied expressions on the team's faces were any indication.

Olivia, Leo, and Gracie quietly pulled out chairs and sat down in the back of the room. The door opened a moment later and Jessica walked back in, retaking her seat toward the front of the table.

"What do you guys think?" Ryan asked, hands folded over his chest as he rocked back on his heels. He caught Olivia's eye for a moment. "My feeling is that if Nicky makes good on his promise to fix things, we should back off."

"Agreed," Aiyana said promptly, as several others around the table nodded.

Jessica raised her hand.

Ryan frowned. "You don't need to raise your hand."

"What about how he ruined the camping trip for everyone?" she asked. "How can he make up for that?"

"Maybe he can ask if we can reschedule it," Abby suggested. "I know we're all disappointed we had to leave."

Everyone nodded and then Jordan spoke up.

"What if Nicky doesn't do what he's promised?" he asked. "Or if he just apologizes to some people and not others?"

"He'll hold up his end of the bargain," Olivia said and Gracie nodded. "And—"

"But wait, what if he doesn't?" Ryan asked. Gracie thought they had Ryan firmly on their side, but he seemed easily swayed, his voice now full of doubt.

Gracie was about to answer when Aiyana spoke up.

"I get the concern but let's give him a week and see where things are at," she said. "We can do an inventory, check in with everyone, and if Nicky hasn't been true to his word, we still have all the info you gathered and can always post stuff later."

"Okay, yeah, that sounds good," Ryan said, his face relaxing. "We can give him the benefit of the doubt."

Gracie smiled with relief, grateful to Aiyana for coming up with such a reasonable compromise.

"So let me tell you what else is going on," Olivia

said, standing up and taking over the meeting. While she spoke, Gracie looked intently around the table, trying to discern if anyone seemed guilty or shifty—Joe and Bryce in particular. But mostly they just looked shocked at what Olivia was saying.

". . . not fair and—" Olivia was interrupted by the door swinging open once more.

They all turned as Chloe walked in, then stopped, her face turning scarlet as she realized they were all staring.

"Sorry," she half whispered. "Ryan said I could come."

He nodded, Chloe sat, and Olivia continued.

"Who's behind this?" Ryan asked angrily the moment Olivia finished explaining the spear-phishing setup.

The room was silent. Gracie stared at Bryce, who seemed shell-shocked, and Joe, who was shaking his head like he couldn't believe it. Did this mean they were innocent? Or just really good at looking innocent? It was turning out that reading the room was hard. She glanced at Leo, who caught her eye and shrugged. Gracie went back to examining the faces around the table, trying to detect any hint of deceit, but everyone just looked confused. Maybe no one here *had* done it.

"Listen, I was really angry at Nicky, you guys know that, but I'd never do something dishonest," Abby said.

"He did bad stuff to people so someone's clearly after him," Aiyana said, rubbing her chin.

Others were nodding.

"Remember when we had to cancel the field trip to Lane Sanctuary last year because someone snuck onto the PA system and made farting noises and no one fessed up so we all got punished?" Joe asked bitterly. "Someone being Nicky, obviously." Joe was on the basketball team and wore his jersey everywhere. Gracie was surprised he cared about a visit to hang out with animals—he always seemed so sports focused—but it was sweet.

"Like losing the camping trip this year," Jessica said, her fingers still playing with her hair.

There it was again, at the edge of Gracie's brain, tingling.

"And when we couldn't do any more science labs last year because he started a fire in a Bunsen burner," Jordan said, obviously still bitter about it and understandably—labs were way more fun than reading about chemical formulas.

"Yeah, but here's the thing," Aiyana said, holding up a hand. "None of that makes it okay for someone to frame him for a crime he didn't commit."

As everyone agreed heartily with this, Gracie tugged at the tingle, trying to see what it was. She looked around the room, and her eyes landed on Jessica, who was nodding as Jordan spoke about how the spear phishing crossed a line. She seemed in full agreement as she pulled, strangely aggressively, on a lock of hair.

Her hair.

Gracie remembered Jessica's face moments ago in the bathroom mirror. As she thought about it again, it was envy that she saw in Jessica's eyes as she stared at Gracie's long hair, hair that was as long as Jessica's had always been until—

And there it was. The tingle became an electric charge zipping through her whole body. Gracie's hands shook.

"It was you," she said forcefully, pointing at Jessica and cutting off Jordan.

Everyone in the room turned to stare at Gracie but she was only looking at one person.

"I don't know what you're talking about," Jessica said, now smoothing her hair as she feigned innocence.

"Wait, you think *Jessica* is framing Nicky?" Ryan asked. "Why?"

"She's good at computers," Gracie began.

Jessica snorted. "That's everyone in this room."

She sounded so certain Gracie felt a new flicker— a flicker of doubt. Was she wrong about this? How awful would that be?

But then Olivia spoke, once again having Gracie's back when it mattered most. "You hate Nicky," she said to Jessica.

Jessica looked at Olivia as if she'd lost it. "Um, yeah, like everyone else in this room and at school."

"He ruined your hair," Gracie said, trying to remember the details of what had happened that day last spring when Nicky had wrapped a lock of Jessica's hair in gum so tightly it had to be cut off, leaving a bald spot that had only begun to grow over.

Jessica shrugged. "He's done awful things to everyone."

"But you said you'd get him back." It was Leo, also stepping up for Gracie when she needed it. "I was there when he did it."

"Me too," Aiyana said slowly. "You said he'd pay."

Jessica bit her lip but this time did not respond.

"You had the access," Olivia said, her voice stormy. "You're Mr. Simmons's aide. Nicky was one of the students who brought in his personal computer when it was allowed—you could have easily looked up his password on the tech log when Mr. Simmons was distracted or left the room."

"Or tried to beak into his house," said Leo.

Gracie felt the energy in the room shift, an intensity building as everyone turned to look at Jessica.

"Are they right?" Ryan asked, his face still disbelieving. "Is it you?"

Jessica looked around the room and slowly narrowed her eyes. "Even if it was, which it wasn't, you'll never prove it."

They'd done it, they'd found the phisher! But she was right—they had no proof and clearly she wasn't going to confess.

"Nicky doesn't deserve this," Olivia fumed.

"Who are you to decide that?" Jessica burst out, poison laced through the words. "He made my life hell—I still get naked mole rat memes! And I'm hardly the only one he's hurt. You better believe he has this coming." She gave them an arch look. "I'm grateful for whoever took matters into their own hands and did it. Honestly, I think he's getting off easy."

"Are you kidding?" Leo asked, eyes wide as he blinked at her. "He could get in trouble with the police."

"Good," Jessica said, standing up. "I hope he does."

"Jessica, this isn't fair," Ryan said. He looked at her as if she was a stranger, someone he was seeing for the very first time. Which was how Gracie was feeling too.

"For real, don't do it," Aiyana added.

"Be the person we know you can be!" Abby added, wringing her hands.

But Jessica gave them all a look of scorn. "Nicky's getting justice," she said. "He's going down, just like the Clarksdale hacker did, and I can't wait." Her parting tone was vicious as she wrenched the door open and stomped out.

Gracie's head was spinning. Once again they had solved the mystery only to be presented with a new one. Because who could possibly stop Jessica's scheme now?

"Is she right? Is there really no way to prove it's her?" Leo asked.

The members of the tech team looked around the table and one by one shook their heads. "This is sophisticated stuff," Jordan said. "A master hacker could take it on but I don't think even Mr. Simmons has those skills."

"So you can't cancel the email?" Olivia asked the other tech team members desperately.

Once again they slowly shook their heads.

"It's too high-level," Bryce said. "We'd need someone as good as the Clarksdale hacker to stop that hack."

"Well, then," Chloe said, pausing as everyone turned to her, and then smiled. "It's a good thing she's here."

It was pin-drop quiet and then the group erupted.

"*You?* But you don't even have a phone!" Leo exclaimed.

Chloe rolled her eyes. "Are you kidding? I'm never getting my phone or laptop back—my mom is going to be holding those forever after what happened at my old school."

"So that's why you come to the library to use the computer," Ryan said.

Chloe nodded. "Yeah, but my mom has a deal with Ms. MacCullough that my history gets tracked every time I'm there. That's why I could never help you with the list."

Gracie understood these questions but they were nothing compared with the real question. "Why did you hack your school computer when you lived in Clarksdale?" she asked, cutting off both Olivia and Bryce. They were instantly still as everyone once more faced Chloe.

She sighed. "Because I was an idiot," she said. "I have mad computer skills and I was taking all these online classes for college kids on cybersecurity—which is basically learning how to hack. I didn't have friends but these girls who were really popular found out about what I could do and pretended they liked me to get me to hack into the system and change their grades so they wouldn't get cut from the JV cheer squad." She sighed again. "Pathetic, I know. I've been talking to a counselor about it for months and I get how dumb it was. But I can't go back to Clarksdale for obvious reasons, so I've been trying to figure out where Nicky is to see if I can save my mom's job."

Gracie's body was limp in the chair as she absorbed all this. Some pieces fit—why Chloe kept turning up all day and why she needed the library computer. But most of it exploded Gracie's brain because she'd never have guessed Chloe had a story like this. Of course, one thing she'd learned today was that everyone had a story—but still, Chloe's was a whopper.

"If Nicky comes back now, will your mom keep her job?" Leo asked. He looked slightly shell-shocked but was the first in the room to recover, of course, because Leo was ever curious. And Gracie realized that was one of the things she liked about him.

"I'm not sure," Chloe said, her mouth turning down. "But I figure the sooner he's found, the better her chances."

"So you'll help him with the phishing email?" Olivia asked, her palms pressed together as she gazed at Chloe.

"Yes," Chloe said, wiggling her fingers. "Get me to a secure computer and I'll get on it. And just so you know, I'd do it no matter what. You guys are right—Nicky doesn't need more grief, not if he's sorry for his past and ready to make up for it."

There was sadness in her voice and Gracie realized it must be hard for Chloe to live down her own past mistakes.

"Fantastic!" Olivia said, pulling out her phone to text Nicky. Gracie was still adjusting to Olivia's transformation from Nicky hater to Nicky supporter—his biggest supporter—but it was a change Gracie respected. Olivia was honest to a fault and a bit short-tempered, but she was fair and quite possibly the most bighearted person Gracie had ever met, next to Mina. Olivia just hid it a little better. And all these things were why Gracie had come to care so much about Olivia over the course of a single day.

"Tell him to come help me," Chloe said. "It'll be faster and easier if we work together."

"Will do," Olivia said, fingers tapping at her screen. "He has a computer you can use too."

Leo was frowning. "What about Jessica? Is she just going to get away with trying to do this?"

"Can you prove she was behind it?" Aiyana asked Chloe.

Chloe looked at Leo, then Gracie, and then Olivia. And then she spoke. "I think foiling her plan is enough," she said. "And now we know what she's capable of—she won't try something like this again."

That was true—especially once she found out the Clarksdale hacker had moved to town.

While Olivia set things up with Nicky, Jordan came over to Gracie and Leo. "You guys seriously tracked Nicky down when the police couldn't do it?"

The rush of sweetness that fizzed up inside Gracie surprised her—but then again, why wouldn't she be proud of herself? It *was* pretty cool.

"Yup," she said, corners of her mouth turning up slightly as she watched Jordan shake his head, clearly impressed.

"And here I thought you were just Mina's shadow," Jordan said, apparently unaware of how rude that was. Gracie had never been anyone's shadow! At least not all the time. Actually, maybe he had a point. Maybe Gracie had been hiding behind her friend. "But it turns out you're some kind of superhero detective."

"She is," Leo agreed. "Put Gracie and her supercharged skills on the case and it's solved, just like that."

"Good stuff," Aiyana said, grinning at Gracie as she and Bryce came over. Aiyana had never talked to her before. Jordan or Bryce either, outside of group work or asking about homework or mentioning her hair. Gracie had always assumed no one was interested in knowing her, but maybe they'd never had a chance—and maybe that was on her. It was something to think about. But no matter how it *had* been, Gracie was glad it was changing.

"Thanks," she said to Aiyana. "I thought it was pretty great when you and your friends got the school cafeteria to set up a composting bin."

Aiyana's grin widened. "We're working on getting a plot for a garden next spring," she said. "You guys should help."

Gracie nodded. "I'd like that."

She was still smiling as Jordan, Bryce, and Aiyana headed toward the door.

"You were just saying that to be nice, right?" Leo asked, his nose wrinkled. "Who wants to garden, with all the snakes and spiders?"

Gracie laughed. "I might," she said. Because she'd never considered it until now—she hadn't considered a lot of things. But that was going to change.

"I don't see it," Olivia said, walking up and putting her phone back into her pocket. "Think of all the smells in a garden."

Gracie had not considered that and was rather touched Olivia had. Her friends knew her!

"Oh, good point," Leo said, sounding relieved. "I didn't want us to all have to join the garden club."

"Why would we all have to join?" Gracie asked as they started toward the door of conference room one.

"Duh, we need something so we can hang out together," he said.

The sweet fizzy feeling was back.

"We could start a speed-skating club," Olivia suggested.

"I don't skate," Gracie said.

Both Leo and Olivia froze. "How is that possible?" Leo asked. "This is hockey country."

"None of us even play hockey," Gracie pointed out.

"I do," Leo sulked.

"So I guess we'll have to start with skating lessons," Olivia said.

Gracie had never been interested in skating but at

this point anything was possible, as long as it didn't smell bad.

They waved to Lucy and Ms. MacCullough, then stepped outside into the late-afternoon sun. The breeze was cool on Gracie's cheeks.

"You guys did it." Ryan was standing with Bryce by one of the purple benches they'd sat on hours earlier, when things were so very different. "You found Nicky and then you found out who was planning to mess up his life and stopped her. I'd say that's a pretty good day."

Gracie had to agree—it had been a good day. A very good day.

"Yeah, Nicky's meeting Chloe and then he'll go to the police," Olivia said. "And he's calling his mom too, so she can stop worrying."

"I hope Ms. Becker keeps her job," Ryan said. "But at least she has a shot at it, thanks to you."

"You guys should start a detective agency," Bryce added.

Olivia rolled her eyes. "In Snow Valley? Nothing mysterious ever happens here. This was just a fluke."

Gracie's phone vibrated in her pocket and she pulled it out.

Where have u been???

It was from Mina.

U said you'd come over ages ago!!! U better have a good excuse.

Gracie grinned. Did she ever!

Coming soon. U will never believe what happened today.

"So true," Leo said. Gracie realized he'd been reading her text over her shoulder. She gave him a sour look as she tucked her phone away but she was grinning.

"What's true?" Olivia asked as they strolled down the path, relaxed together for the first time all day.

"That this day was unbelievable," Gracie said. She was tired but in a satisfying way, the way she felt after a long day of skiing or swimming in the lake—like she had used her mind and body for good things and now it was time to rest.

Olivia slung one arm over Gracie's shoulder, the other over Leo's. "That it was," she said. "That it was."

EPILOGUE

Snippet from the Snow Valley Police Department Log

Missing Persons Case 3125

Nicholas Finley

Mr. Finley was reported missing from a school camping trip at approximately 6:05 a.m. Saturday morning. He was found that same Saturday evening, less than twenty-four hours after the report was filed.

Mr. Finley arrived at the station of his own volition, claiming to have been unaware there was concern for his whereabouts. He had gone on a morning walk without informing a teacher and gotten lost. He apologized for the misunderstanding and any confusion he had caused.

Mr. Finley was reunited with his mother, Shari Jones, at approximately 5:14 p.m.

As Mr. Finley had sustained no injury and

*appeared in excellent spirits, he was released into his
mother's care.*

<small>CASE STATUS: CLOSED</small>

**Snippet from the Snow Valley Secondary Winter Club
Listings:**

<small>CLUB NAME: ALL LEVEL SKATING FOR FUN</small>

Members: *Leo Harper-Jones, Olivia Montgomery,
Grace O'Brian, Chloe Becker, Nicky Finley, Mina Li,
Bryce Jacobs, Jordan Smith*

Advisor: *Ms. Becker, seventh-grade English teacher*

ACKNOWLEDGMENTS

This book is its best self because of the amazing Emily Seife, whose ideas, edits, and feedback made it the book I envisioned but could not have created on my own. I won the editor lottery with Emily, along with the terrific team at Scholastic: editorial assistant Kassy Lopez, production editor Janell Harris, cover designer Maeve Norton, publicist Brooke Shearouse, copy editor Priscilla Eakeley, and proofreaders Lara Kennedy, Nicole Ortiz, and Catherine Weening.

I am forever grateful to be represented by the incomparable Sara Crowe, best agent in the business, who works with the best crew in the business, Pippin Properties, aka the Pips: Holly, Elena, Ashley, Marissa, and Morgan. You guys are the true dream team!

To ensure I honored the relationship Olivia has with Benji, I got added feedback from the compassionate, wise, and incredibly insightful Jenny Licata.

My books and my life are better because of the wonderful people who read my stories, brainstorm ideas with me, and know when to be honest or when to just say nice things: Marianna Baur, Kira Bazile, Donna

Freitas, Lisa Graff, Deb Heiligman, Leslie Margolis, Carolyn MacCullough, Debbi Michiko Florence, Marie Rutkowski, Jill Santopolo, Eliot Schrefer, Rebecca Stead, and Martin Wilson. I am one lucky duck to have you all in my life.

Some people find one really awesome job, but I've had the great fortune to find two. When I'm not writing I am a librarian at P.S. 32 in Brooklyn, working with students I adore and learning from teachers and administrators at the top of their game. Denise Watson, Stephen Grecco, Perniece Roper, Ms. Ming, Ms. Johnson, and Ms. Lisa, thank you for your endless support, shared wisdom, and excellent humor.

I also hit the jackpot with family. My sister, Sam, is a supremely wonderful human and fiercely loving advocate of children, and I am grateful she's my team-mate for life. Hugs, kisses, and so much love for my four most fabulous nephews, Dash, Shiloh, Avi, and Khai, and for Nghia, who is the brother I always wanted. My nest emptied this year as my two little ones somehow got big and headed off to college, but they are in my heart no matter how far they go, and it is a supreme joy to be their mom. And last but never least is Greg, the guy who shares my empty nest, listens as I talk through story ideas, and sends me many pictures of the cat when I am away. I love you all.

ABOUT THE AUTHOR

Daphne Benedis-Grab is the author of the middle grade thrillers *I Know Your Secret, I Know You're Lying,* and *I Will Find You.* She is the part-time school librarian at P.S. 32 in Brooklyn, where she gets to hang out with kids and books all day (she is a very lucky person!). She lives in New York City with her husband, two teens, and a cat who has been known to sit on her computer if he feels she has been typing too long. Visit her at daphnebg.com.

"Do exactly what I say, when I say it, or I will reveal your secret."

TURN THE PAGE FOR A SNEAK PEEK OF
I KNOW YOUR SECRET!

CHAPTER 1

SUNDAY: 5:30 P.M.
OWEN

It was random that Owen even checked his email before dinner that Sunday. Usually he went straight from pickup basketball with the guys to the backyard. His stepdad, Big Rob, was still insisting it was warm enough for Sunday night barbecues. Which was fine with Owen—give him a pile of ribs soaked in Big Rob's secret Lexington sauce and he would be happy eating outside in January. But Mom said barbecue season in upstate New York ended with the first frost—which had been that morning.

So when Owen got home, Big Rob was standing next to the cold grill, saying, "It was more a light dusting of rain, not an actual frost," while Mom countered that rain did not leave a white icy residue.

Owen figured it would be a while before the family ate anything, so he went into Mom's office to use the computer. His older sister, Mina (who was technically his stepsister), normally hogged it, but Mina was on a college tour with her mom and away for the week. So the computer was free for Owen and the project he had started during the Covid-19 shutdown.

It wasn't something he had told anyone—right now it was just his. But Owen was creating a graphic novel. None of his friends were into comics, drawing, or writing, and while Big Rob was enthused about most of Owen's interests, Mom and Dad were more invested in Owen's grades, which were somewhat less than great. They didn't nag him much, but Owen knew they might butt in if they realized that half the time they thought Owen was doing homework, he was actually working on his story.

Owen had reached a point in the book where he needed to know a little more about the armor worn by samurai for when his character went back in time. He did a quick search, found some great images, and then, while they were printing, logged into his account.

And that was how he ended up being the first of the four to see the email.

GEMMA

"Can I please be excused?" Gemma asked, doing her best to appear casual. This was hard because she was pretty much crawling out of her skin. But it was essential that Mom not see how desperate Gemma was to get on her phone after Mom's new "screen-free Sundays." Mom was still scarred by all the screen time Gemma, Kate, and Avi had had during the Covid-19 shutdown. Although it'd been necessary for school and to socialize online, now that things were open again and people could go out, Gemma's mom was determined to keep them off screens as much as possible.

"Isn't it your night to load the dishwasher?" Gemma's evil younger sister, Kate, asked.

"No, it's Avi's," Gemma said between gritted teeth. Her older brother, who was as sweet as Kate was evil, nodded cheerfully.

"Okay, then," Mom said, sounding reluctant.

"I did all my homework," Gemma said, smiling

like she wasn't aching to snatch her phone out of the charging cabinet and fly up to her room.

"Great, off you go," Dad said, waving Gemma toward the living room.

It took everything in her but she managed to walk calmly to the cabinet, take out the phone without checking it (Mom was watching), and meander to the stairs. She didn't start running until she was half-way up and Kate had started moaning about how she hated her math teacher.

And after all that? *He* hadn't even texted.

Gemma threw herself down on her pink comforter-covered bed (so immature, but Mom wouldn't get her a new one until high school, which was years away) and scrolled through her notifications, then went to her inbox. She noticed the email right away and not because the subject line was all caps. Gemma noticed it right away because of what it said.

I KNOW YOUR SECRET

7:17 P.M.
TODD

Todd wanted to punch the computer screen.

He could imagine how it would feel to put his fist through the screen, blasting that email apart—but obviously he didn't. Mom was so proud of the old desktop her boss had given her that it sat in a place of honor on the kitchen table where they ate. Todd knew Mom's boss just wanted to get rid of the computer without hassle since it was ancient, but the important thing was that Mom didn't know that. And it did still work. Even though it took up half the small table in their very small trailer.

"I forgot my milk," Mom said, coming out of her bedroom. She was getting ready to watch her Sunday shows.

Todd quickly closed the email before she could see what was on the screen.

"You know how it helps me relax." She was wearing what she called her "cozy robe," her feet in the bunny slippers Todd had gotten her for her birthday. Mom loved bunnies and wore the slippers every night.

"Want me to get it for you?" Todd asked. He started to stand up and found he felt shaky, almost dizzy, from what he'd just read.

"No, you keep doing your work on the computer," Mom said, grabbing a teacup and saucer for her milk. It was the "little touches," as she called them, that made Mom happy. That and anything involving bunnies, Todd, or chocolate.

As soon as Mom was safely back in her room, Todd clicked back to the email. As he read it a second time, his fists clenched up.

But punching wasn't going to help him get out of this:

I know your secret. Do what I say, when I say it, and I won't tell a soul. Skip even one step and I will tell everyone. Text me at this number as soon as you read this email. And then get ready for tomorrow. It's going to be a very big day.

Ally's hands were shaking, her breath coming in short, sharp bursts as she shoved things around on her desk, trying to find her phone so she could send the text. Thank goodness she had checked her email tonight! It had been a long day helping Grandpa and Gram— Sundays were always long days, not that Ally minded. Nothing mattered more to her than the animals at the sanctuary she helped her grandparents run. And nothing made her, or her grandparents, happier.

But still, the work was tiring. Often after evening animal feeding and cuddles, Ally took a long, hot shower, fell into bed with a book, and passed out by nine. And what if she had done that tonight and missed this email?

It was too awful to even contemplate.

She finally found her phone, wedged into a far corner of the desk under a pile of *Cat Care* magazines. It took two tries to open up a new message and type in the phone number from the email. Then she hesitated. What was the proper response when someone was blackmailing you? She settled on *It's Ally* and pressed send. Then she waited, cold sweat slithering down her sides, staring at her phone.

Ally had no idea who could be threatening her like this. And how had they found out her secret? It was most certainly the one thing Ally never, ever wanted anyone to know. Because if anyone found out what she had done—

Her stomach tumbled ominously as a bubble appeared on the screen, three dots flashing. Ally closed her eyes and said a quick prayer. This person—whoever they were—had the power to ruin everything Ally had ever truly loved.